"There is nothing crazy about wanting a child," she protested.

"Why shouldn't I want to have a baby on my own?"

"Because you have no possible conception of what it will be like raising one by yourself," Jacob replied. "And I should know," he practically whispered.

"I know that you love Cody and want the best of everything for him. Can't you understand that I want to feel those same feelings? That I want to have someone of my own to love?"

Her voice died away in the stillness as Sasha realized exactly what she had said. She'd admitted that she was lonely and alone in a world where love was the magic password to happiness. And she had admitted it to a single man who had told her many times that he had no desire for a wife.

Please, please don't let Jacob know that I'd give anything to have Cody for a son...and him for a husband.

Dear Reader,

Unforgettable Bride, by bestselling author Annette Broadrick, is May's VIRGIN BRIDES selection, *and* the much-requested spin-off to her DAUGHTERS OF TEXAS series. Rough, gruff rodeo star Bobby Metcalf agreed to a quickie marriage—sans honeymoon!—with virginal Casey Carmichael. But four years later, he's still a married man—one intent on being a husband to Casey in every sense....

Fabulous author Arlene James offers the month's FABULOUS FATHERS title, *Falling for a Father of Four.* Orren Ellis was a single dad to a brood of four, so hiring sweet Mattie Kincaid seemed the perfect solution. Until he found himself falling for this woman he could never have.... Stella Bagwell introduces the next generation of her bestselling TWINS ON THE DOORSTEP series. In *The Rancher's Blessed Event,* an ornery bronc rider must open his heart both to the woman who'd betrayed him...and her child yet to be born.

Who can resist a sexy, stubborn cowboy—particularly when he's your husband? Well, Taylor Cassidy tries in Anne Ha's *Long, Tall Temporary Husband.* But will she succeed? And Sharon De Vita's irresistible trio, LULLABIES AND LOVE, continues with *Baby with a Badge,* where a bachelor cop finds a baby in his patrol car...and himself in desperate need of a woman's touch! Finally, new author C.J. Hill makes her commanding debut with a title that sums it up best: *Baby Dreams and Wedding Schemes.*

Romance has everything you need from new beginnings to tried-and-true favorites. Enjoy each and every novel this month, and every month!

Warm Regards!

Joan Marlow Golan

Joan Marlow Golan
Senior Editor, Silhouette Romance

Please address questions and book requests to:
Silhouette Reader Service
U.S.: 3010 Walden Ave., P.O. Box 1325, Buffalo, NY 14269
Canadian: P.O. Box 609, Fort Erie, Ont. L2A 5X3

BABY DREAMS AND WEDDING SCHEMES

C.J. Hill

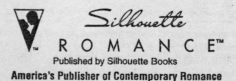

Silhouette
ROMANCE™
Published by Silhouette Books
America's Publisher of Contemporary Romance

My deepest thanks to three Fairy Godpeople:

Melissa Jeglinski: For a golden opportunity.
My sister Judy: The original Bednobs and Broomsticks.
Barry: For repeating three little words whenever
I needed them: "So, do it."
I did!

 SILHOUETTE BOOKS

ISBN 0-373-19299-1

BABY DREAMS AND WEDDING SCHEMES

Copyright © 1998 by Lois Richer

C.J. HILL,

who also writes as Lois Richer for Steeple Hill's Love Inspired line, was born and raised in a small town in western Canada and could hardly wait to get out in the big, wide world. Once there, she earned her bachelor's degree, started a career and searched high and low to find fame and fortune. Eventually she returned "home." It's that same small town where she met her husband and today raises her two sons. The wonderful sense of community and closeness found in rural areas is what she loves to explore in her stories.

Her family has come to understand that books, the computer and Mom are invisibly linked. C.J. admits that her ideas often overtake her time and shelf space. And so, when all else fails, the family dog takes her for a walk in the woods, where they discuss her next project. They'd both be pleased to hear from you at: Box 639, Nipawin, Saskatchewan, Canada S0E 1E0

Dear Reader,

Welcome to my very first book for Silhouette Romance. I'm thrilled to be part of this wonderful tradition of love stories that tug at the heart and remind us all of the most important things in life. If you're like me, you enjoy reading novels that take you away from your daily problems and plunge you into the wonders of that "special" love. When you're there, anything can happen, and frequently does! And that's why I wrote *Baby Dreams and Wedding Schemes*. I hope you enjoy this book and that you find a refreshing new way to look at your own life.

May your days be filled with joy and much love.

C J Hill.

P.S. I'd love to have you check out my titles in the new Love Inspired line, too. Look for the FAITH, HOPE AND CHARITY series in a bookstore near you.

Chapter One

"You lied!"

"That squeaky little voice could penetrate steel," Sasha Lambert muttered, gritting her teeth and trying to remain calm.

Warning—this is what cute, darling little babies grow into. Rethink your plan! There it was again; that ridiculously mocking voice inside her head issuing its gloomy admonition.

I am just as capable as the next woman when it comes to children. I merely need to apply the fine art of reason to this situation, she told herself.

"Look, little boy," she coaxed quietly. "I can't have a funeral for Henry in my store! I don't do funerals."

He stared up at her, his eyes wide and accusatory. One short, stubby finger pointed to the sign in her window. "My dad tol' me that sign says you can do anything here."

Sasha sighed once in resignation, the second time in capitulation as she spotted one fat tear suspended on the end of his incredibly long lashes. "Actually it says we cater to all occasions. But it's wrong. Sorry. No funeral. No way."

She hadn't meant to say it quite so loudly, but the words rang through Bednobs and Broomsticks like a cowbell on the open prairie. The customers quietly browsing her craft store opened their eyes wide to frown at the tall, slim woman positioned near the half-finished train display in the main aisle.

Sasha ignored them all, examining the preschooler from her impressive height. He refused to budge. Instead he stood watching her, his big brown eyes now welling with tears.

"But we hafta," he wailed as one glistening droplet finally plopped down onto the copper freckles covering his chubby cheeks. "My dad's gonna kill me when he finds out and then I'll get grounded. I just gotta have Henry's funeral first."

She tried to ignore the sympathy pangs that were mounting inside her mushy heart. The frosty looks of condemnation her customers were casting her way didn't help stifle the gnawing sense of censure that yawned inside. Nor the pangs of regret. Her eyes fell on the bit of paper she had taped to the counter.

"Word for the day. Compunction: anxiety arising from guilt." Stupid word! Who needed extra guilt?

Some mother you'll make, her subconscious chided. *No empathy.* She frowned, glaring maliciously at the cash register. She was as empathetic as the next woman and she fully intended to be the best mother since sliced bread. So there!

Sasha tossed her shining head back and considered her folly in moving to Allen's Springs, Montana. Was it her fault poor old Henry had died right here in the middle of the store? she demanded of herself.

"I'm sure your father will understand when you explain it all to him." There, her voice was kind but firm.

"Nah, he won't." The face drooped with misery. "He never does. He's gonna be really mad. I just know it."

Sasha closed her eyes in defeat as the tentacles of his mournful distress squeezed tightly around her heartstrings. With difficulty, she repressed the urge to push back the tumble of brown curls from his brow.

Softie. Don't get involved. Not today. You've got that appointment to prepare for. If you're lucky, you'll soon have your own kids to worry about.

''Well,'' she said in capitulation, knowing darn well she never took her own advice, ''perhaps if I spoke to your father.'' She glanced around the empty store and made a face. ''I don't think anyone else is coming in today anyway. That announcement of mine pretty well cleared everyone out.'' She smiled grimly.

At least he had the grace to look downcast at her loss of business. Sasha handed him a tissue.

''Here. Blow.'' Her tone was filled with resignation. ''What's your father's name?''

''No! You can't!'' The boy's voice trembled with fear. ''I—I'll tell him myself.'' He was backing down the aisle toward the door now, one knobby knee showing through the wide tear in his black pants.

Sasha was amazed. What kind of an ogre was the child's father, for heaven's sake, to engender such fear in the boy? And where was he when his son needed him? This was the fifth time in as many days that she'd had the child as an afternoon visitor. Alone.

She darted past him and whipped the door closed, sending the chimes tinkling throughout the empty aisles. That was one advantage of having very long legs. She could outrun almost everyone. Of course, at five feet eleven and seven-eighths inches she also towered above every other living soul.

''I think you and I had better have a talk,'' Sasha told him firmly as she closed her hand around one thin shoulder. ''Come on. I made cookies yesterday.'' He looked doubtful. ''Triple chocolate chip with nuts.''

That seemed to decide the issue. He trailed along behind her, his black leather shoes clicking against the worn oak planks of the floor.

Black leather shoes?

Sasha took a second look at the child and grimaced. Most of the kids in Allen's Springs wore jeans and a T-shirt with sneakers. This child was distinctly out of place in his white shirt, dress pants and leather shoes; the very same items he'd worn each time he'd visited her.

"What's your name?" Sasha asked softly, leading him through the connecting door to her small living quarters at the rear. Somehow they had never gotten 'round to introductions.

"Cody," he told her, gazing around with interest. "Is this where you live? I like it."

His chubby fingers twiddled with the stuffed parrot that hung behind her sofa. "Trains," he crowed, his eyes sparkling as he moved toward the display in the center of her living room.

Sasha watched as he lovingly gazed at the miniature machines, reached out a tentative hand and then dropped it back by his side. His eyes were huge, round saucers as he studied the red locomotives sitting silent on the tracks she had tacked to a board late last night.

"Four," he half whispered to himself, nodding. "Here's the engine and the c'boose. This one is for carrying stuff."

Sasha pondered his rapt expression as she lifted the jug of milk from the refrigerator and poured a glass for herself and one for the child. Cody seemed mesmerized by her newest project. Good. The boy's interest boded well for her expansion plans.

Sasha grinned as she removed several of the biggest cookies from the nutcracker cookie jar on her counter and arranged them on a tray. As the eldest of six children, if there was one thing she had experience in, it was kids and what they liked. Sasha grimaced. She should know; she'd played both mother and father in her own family for years.

The fact that this child was a little different from any of the children she'd baby-sat through high school and college just meant she needed a break from work. To get back her perspective! she told herself.

"Let's have our snack in the backyard," she told him, pushing the screen door open with one hip as she carried out the tray. "Then we'll talk about Henry."

At the mention of that name, Cody's round face fell and he followed her out the door onto a tiny patch of lawn. "Henry's gone," he muttered disconsolately. "I didn't mean to hurt him. I just wanted to take him for a walk."

Sasha's motherly heart ached at the sadness in his tone. Poor little waif.

"I was ever so careful to lift him gently."

"Well, it was a nice idea, Cody, but I don't think goldfish go for walks. They like their bowls."

He shook his head sadly. "Doesn't matter," he whispered. "Everything dies." It was a solemn denunciation of his whole five-year-old world.

Sasha ruffled his hair gently, enjoying the feel of those silky strands against her palms.

"Who else died?" she asked, waiting for him to look at her.

He didn't. Instead one grubby fist dashed away the tears before he picked up one of her cookies and started chewing. His voice was quiet when he spoke. "Rocket."

"Who's Rocket?"

"My dog, o' course." Cody peered up at her then, as if to assess her mental age. "He got hit by a car when I letted him out of the gate." He sniffed sadly. "An' George and Gertrude."

Sasha frowned. His grandparents?

"How did they die?" she asked softly.

"Ate too much." He picked up a second cookie while his other hand grasped the glass.

Sasha was mystified. "Ate too much?" She tried to play along. Maybe this having kids thing was harder than she thought. "But that wasn't your fault. People feed themselves. Except for babies, of course. No one could blame you, Cody."

He shook his head doubtfully. "I feeded them too much birdseed." His mouth was stuffed full of cookie and Sasha wasn't sure she heard him correctly.

"Birdseed?"

He nodded. "Uh-huh. And I didn't keep their cage clean 'nuf, neither." Sadly, he scuffed his toe on the grass. "Dad said you can't be pushing stuff at canaries all the time. They like to be left alone. Gertrude stopped singing one day and then she got dead."

A smile twitched at the corners of her mouth as Sasha realized her error.

"And is that all?" she asked, unable to resist brushing her hand over his darkly shining head once more.

"Nope." He slurped down the rest of the milk and then leaned over to pick a dandelion.

"Who else?"

His brown eyes peered up into hers. "Shelley—that was my turtle. And Rolly."

"Who's Rolly?" She was almost afraid to hear the answer.

"Gerbil," he told her succinctly. "Got out of the cage and Dad stepped on him. Axidennnally, o' course."

"Oh, of course." Sasha smiled, watching the round face with a pang. He looked so forlorn as he recounted the death of all his little pets.

"Henry was 'sposed to be my last chance. Now he's dead, too. Just like my mom."

It came out of left field, knocking her back in her chair.

"Your mom," she half whispered, shocked by his bald statement. "What happened to your mom?"

He sniffed loudly. "She got dead, too." He bent his head, shifting away from her probing glance.

"Was she sick?" Sasha hated asking the questions but for some reason she just had to know how this little scrap of a child came to be without a mother.

"Uh-uh. Least, I don't think so. She got dead from a gun."

"Oh, Cody." Her soft heart melted then and she cuddled the wiggling little sweat-scented body close to her abundant chest. "I'm so sorry, sweetheart. A mommy's an awful thing for a boy to lose."

He hugged her back tightly, sniffing at the threatening deluge of tears. When at last he pushed away, Sasha let him go with an empty ache in her heart and her arms.

"It's okay," he mumbled. "'Sides, she's in heaven now." He cocked his head to one side. "Do you know, 'bout heaven?" he demanded, wiping one sleeve across his nose as he frowned up at her.

Sasha smiled. "Yes, I do. And I think your mom is very happy there."

His big eyes studied her speculatively for a moment. "I guess."

"But it still hurts, doesn't it?" she guessed.

"Yeah." He nodded glumly. "My mom used to laugh all the time. We had fun and we had lots of good times together. She always had surprises for me. Now we never have them. My dad doesn't talk about her no more."

"Why, Cody?" It was an invasion of privacy and under any other circumstances Sasha wouldn't have probed, but there was something about Cody and his sad little face that tugged at her heartstrings, begged her to listen to his childish explanation.

"'Cause it's my fault that she died and he don't want people to blame me, I guess."

"Oh, sweetheart, no. It isn't your fault at all. It couldn't be." Sasha couldn't bear to hear it. She gazed into those trusting brown eyes and the familiar ache for a child of her own welled once more.

Stop it, she ordered her brain. Think about this child for now.

He was watching her, waiting.

"Sometimes God just wants people to go and live with him, honey, and there's nothing we did or can do that will stop that." Sasha had no idea where the words came from but she was thankful Cody seemed to accept them.

His forehead wrinkled in a frown as he considered what she said, as if checking her sincerity. "Are you sure?"

"Absolutely, positively, unfailingly, irrevocably, indubitably sure, Cody."

"I dunno what all that stuff means," he mumbled, his face tipped up so that she could see the light that gleamed in his eyes. "But if you're sure that I didn't do nuthin' bad, I guess that's okay."

With lightning swift change he shifted the conversation mode. "Can I play with those trains?" His head jerked toward the doorway. "I never had no trains to play with before."

Sasha smiled. She was a fool. With his track record in pet care, she shouldn't let him anywhere near the display. Let alone touch it. Nevertheless, she heard herself agree.

"Yes, you can play with them if you treat them very carefully. They're my special trains and they don't like it if you're rough with them. Okay?"

His eyes were as big as saucers at the prospect of handling the models. He nodded his agreement as she led him back inside. Together they maneuvered the huge board outside onto the lush green lawn. Sasha ran an extension cord and tested the entire mechanism.

When his plump little fingers closed around a fire-red

engine, she posed one last question. "What's your dad's name, Cody? I need to call him and tell him you're here."

His big clear eyes stared at her for one long moment, assessing her. Then he shrugged. "His name is Jacob Windsor," he told her proudly. The child's brow furrowed. "He don't like people buggin' him when he's workin' though."

Sasha held her tongue with difficulty. Of all the insensitive brutes! "Well, I have to tell him where you are, Cody," she said with some asperity. "He could be worried."

Doubtful, her mind chided spitefully.

Cody watched her for a moment and then recited his father's phone number with a happy grin. Pleased with his good memory, he turned back to his perusal of her trains.

Sasha squared her shoulders. Jacob Windsor had to be a cold, insensitive man. He sure didn't deserve to have a wonderful son like Cody. How else did one explain a father who would leave a child so floundering, so unsure of his place in the world? This boy needed love and support, not guilt about his mother's death, regardless of what had happened.

She poured herself another glass of milk and considered the situation at hand. It was up to her to rectify the matter, Sasha decided. If the man was so anesthetized to his son's doubts and questions, it was her duty to set Mr. Jacob Windsor straight. The man needed to know his son was in pain and help him alleviate it.

She wasn't surprised when the knock came at the side door fifteen minutes later. A stiff and formal telephone voice had curtly informed her that the Reverend Jacob Windsor would be over immediately to collect Cordell.

But when she opened the door, Sasha lost all ability to converse as she gazed at the very tall, very handsome man who stood waiting.

He's taller than you. Her eyes relayed this unheard-of

information with lightning speed to her foggy brain as Sasha tried to ignore the pulse of awareness thudding through her body.

"I believe my son is here," he said quietly, his voice a low, husky rumble.

"Oh. Uh, yes. Yes, he is. Outside playing." She nodded, holding the door wider.

Get a grip, she ordered her mushy brain. Think of the boy.

"I, um, I wanted to talk to you first, though. I'm Sasha Lambert." She thrust her hand out toward him and was surprised to feel the strength in his lean grip.

He was tall, six three or four at least. And gaunt. That was the only way to describe the jutting bones that carved the aristocratic planes of his rugged face. His jet-black hair flowed away from his forehead with just a tinge of silver visible on the sides. Solemn and sad, gray eyes met hers, cloudy with his own thoughts.

"Jacob Windsor. I'm the new minister at First Avenue."

She digested the news with a nod, motioning to the nearest kitchen chair. Stern and sober; the name suited him and his profession.

"I assume that is your craft store in front," he murmured. "I hope Cody didn't break something." His voice had the wistful tone of a man who knew the truth and wished he didn't.

Sasha glanced down the long, lean length of him, taking note of the old-fashioned trousers and shirt he wore and the shabby jacket with elbow patches. Even so, the man was a hunk.

"I've just made coffee," she offered, forcing herself to smile, hoping to counteract the lack of air in her lungs. "Would you like some?"

"Please don't bother on my account. I'll just take Cody home and leave you in peace."

He turned toward the back door abruptly, causing Sasha to jump in where angels wouldn't have.

"No, please." She grasped his sleeve in her fingers, tugging him away from the screen and Cody's whirring sounds as he ran the engine around the track. "I really do want to talk to you and it would be easier over a cup of coffee, don't you think?"

Those silver gray eyes stared intently at her hand and Sasha pulled it away immediately, as if burned. Jacob Windsor resumed his seat slowly, studying her through narrowed eyes.

"What, exactly, is this about?" he asked, a thread of iron evident in the low rumbling timbre of his voice.

Sasha took another breath and charged in.

"Cody," she told him clearly, setting a steaming mug of coffee and a huge slice of fresh apple pie in front of him. "I want to talk to you about your son."

One black eyebrow lifted as he contemplated the pie and the steaming coffee, but he said not a word. Instead, he picked up a fork and cut off a piece, placing it between his lips like a connoisseur of baking.

"This is delicious," he murmured. "But you don't have to feed me. Widowers get used to fending for themselves." His cool gaze studied her. "That *is* what this is about, isn't it, *Miss* Lambert?"

There was something in his tone that rasped across her nerves. Some hidden meaning behind those innocent words that was meant to stop her from further questions.

Sasha watched the craggy lines of his face harden into a rigid mask.

"You want to help me out by being a mother to my poor, orphaned son." His smile was not friendly. "You want to share some of the load that single parenthood presents. You want to relieve Cody of a father who has abnegated his responsibilities whe—"

"What was that word?"

Sasha grabbed a pad and began to print.

"What word?" His gray eyes glared at her, angry at the interruption.

She ignored the anger. "Ab-something." She glanced up at him. "You said you had ab-something your responsibilities."

"No, Miss Lambert, I did not. I said you *thought* I had abnegated my respon—"

"Could you spell that?"

She heard the sigh. Anyone would have. It was long and drawn out, as if to show the listener what extreme patience he exercised. When her eyes studied his face, she saw a look of disgust there. Loathing, almost.

"Miss Lambert. If we could return to the matter at hand?"

"In a minute." She shook her head. "This is important. Could you please spell that abneg...whatever it was."

He spelled it, slowly and carefully, as if she were mentally deficient and would never be able to print the letters if he spoke in a normal tone.

"Thank you." Sasha grinned and slapped the sticky note against her fridge.

He frowned, glancing from her to the fridge. "What are you doing?"

"Collecting a word for the day," she told him airily, pouring fresh coffee into his empty cup. "I try to get a really good one that I can use all day long." She moved toward the counter to replace the decanter.

"Abnegate." She rolled the word over her tongue to test its flavor. "It means to give up something, right?"

He nodded, dazed by the sudden turn of events.

"Thought so." Sasha grinned. "I can usually tell from the context. Would you like some pie? I don't want to abnegate my responsibilities as hostess." Her dark head tipped back to study his annoyed features. "Now, what were you saying?"

Jacob frowned. ''I can't remember,'' he admitted dryly. ''Do you always go off on these tangents?''

''Yes.'' She grinned.

But Jacob Windsor wasn't watching her. He was glancing around her home. She could easily read the curious thoughts flitting across his expressive face. His wide mouth tipped downward on one side as his eyes remained fixed on the overstuffed purple wing chair she'd recovered herself. Finally they swiveled away from the matching sofa.

''That's a rather, uh, unusual piece of furniture.''

Sasha burst out laughing. She couldn't help it. People in Allen's Springs had been thinking that for years but to date no one had told her outright, to her face.

''I guess I am mercurial,'' she grinned. Then added, ''Some people even say I have rapid and unpredictable changes of mood.''

He nodded slowly. ''Yes,'' he admitted. ''I can see that. Now, about Cody?''

''Oh, Cody! He's a great kid,'' she enthused. ''But he's got a problem.''

Jacob Windsor grinned. At least she thought that's what you could call it. His lips curled in a dry, mirthless sneer that made him look hard as a rock.

''I'm sure he does. More than one, in fact.'' His gray eyes hardened to slits of steel. ''But nothing that I can't deal with. I'm used to it, you see. I am his father, after all.''

''Yes.'' She nodded. ''That is your bailiwick. But I don't think you're handling it very well.''

Black eyebrows tilted upward mockingly. '''Bailiwick'?'' He shook his dark head in amusement. ''Yes, I guess it is.'' His face hardened. ''Look, Miss Lambert. I am perfectly capable of dealing with my son and his problems without the help of a female.''

Sasha decided she didn't like the look he cast her way

but watched silently as he surged to his feet, one hand digging into his pocket.

"We don't need a little mother to take care of us. We're doing just fine. Let me pay you for whatever damage he's done and then we can get on with our respective lives." He thumbed several bills from a worn, tattered leather wallet.

"Will this about cover the damage?"

Sasha shook her head determinedly. "Not nearly," she muttered, frustrated by his uncaring attitude.

Mr. Jacob Windsor merely peeled off a few more dollars, ignoring her sarcasm.

"You know," she mused, head tilted to one side as she perused his rigid stance. "I always thought a minister of the church was supposed to have some special sense that lets him see into the misery and confusion of others, empathize with their troubles. You appear to have lost it where Cody's concerned."

She watched the tide of red rise from the base of his neck to the black roots of his hair.

"Now, just one blasted minute. For an autodidact like yourself—"

"A what?"

His face wore the smug look of one who knows he has the upper hand. "It means a self-taught person."

Sasha could feel him watching her scribble it on another of her sticky notes. She ignored him, finished the word, or a facsimile of it, and smacked it against the refrigerator with a snap of her wrist.

"Yes, I guess I am self-taught," she told him. "That doesn't mean I can ignore what I see. Go on."

He inclined his head, obviously choosing his words with care. "To someone like you, who is a stranger to us and outside of our family, perhaps it seems as if Cody is having difficulties."

He is a blind, narcissistic fool, Sasha decided impartially. Condescending and rude, yes. But still a hunk.

"I assure you that Cody is a perfectly normal little boy who is simply adjusting to a new environment."

Sasha placed her hands on her hips. This was going to be harder than she thought.

"Especially when he thinks he's responsible for his own mother's death, and that you blame him for that?"

He spouted another word Sasha hadn't ever heard before but she had no intention of asking him to repeat it. In fact, she pretended she hadn't heard it as she watched his hands curl into fists at his sides. She faced the flintlike steely gleam in his eyes when they riveted on her.

"What did you say?" His voice was frigid with dislike.

"Cody thinks he's the cause of your wife's death and that you are keeping mum about it to shield him from public opinion."

"Just how did my son come to confide such information?" The words were chipped away from his hard lips as he scowled at her across the table.

"It was after Henry died. You see—"

"Who?" His eyes wore a dark, puzzled look as they met hers.

"Henry. The goldfish. The bag broke and Henry ended up drying out on my floor. He's still there, I guess."

Sasha thought about that for a moment before Jacob Windsor's throat-clearing sounds drew her attention back to him.

"Anyway, Cody wanted me to give Henry a proper funeral. He said you'd kill him for making the mistake of terminating another pet. I don't do funerals—especially goldfish."

"I believe the sign in your window says you cater to all occasions," he said tongue-in-cheek.

Sasha shook her head. "Sorry. Not funerals. But to get

back to Cody..." She purposely let the words hang for emphasis.

"Yes, let's." He was clearly not going to be deterred by her sharp tone.

"In Cody's words, 'everything dies.'" There, she'd said it. Now he would tell her to mind her own business.

But Jacob Windsor just shook his head stupidly. Sasha could see he wasn't following.

"I'm not going to kill Cody just because his goldfish died." He looked confused.

"Oh, good." She sipped at her coffee for a moment, trying to organize her thoughts. It didn't help, so she plunged right in. "Well, anyway, it was during this discussion that Cody told me about his mother dying. He said she died from a gun and that you didn't talk about her any more because you didn't want people to blame him."

"Oh, my Lord. I thought we had left all that behind." It was a groan of despair that touched her nerves as the tall man stooped against the tabletop, head in his hands as he sighed in defeat. "I really hoped he'd forgotten all about it." His voice was full of pain and sadness.

"What happened?" she whispered softly, reaching out to brush her fingers over his arm in empathetic understanding. She pulled back when he flinched. "I just want to help Cody as much as I can."

When he looked up at her his eyes were dark and hooded. He withdrew visibly into a shell that blazed don't touch like a neon sign. The deeply carved lines of his face emphasized the sadness that marked him.

"I'm not sure you can," he whispered hoarsely. His voice was flat. "And if anyone's to blame for Angela's death, it's I. I insisted we go away. Unfortunately, it was too late."

Sasha heard the words in stunned disbelief, but filed them away for later inspection.

"Cody was three when Angela died during our summer

vacation." He was speaking again in a dull, flat monotone. "She'd had an asthma attack. For some reason he'd started having nightmares. He dreams that she was killed by some punks who were trying to steal from the church. He thinks he saw the whole thing."

"Oh, no." Sasha gasped in consternation, imagining the terror such an event must have had on his young mind.

"In fact he did see her choking. But it happened almost three years ago and in another place. I was hoping he'd forget it all. Put it away. Get on with life." He shook his head. "Apparently neither of us can," he half whispered to himself.

Sasha thought for a moment considering the little boy's plight and his words. "The series of recurring problems with pets probably brought on some of his self-blame. He seems to have some difficulty keeping them alive." She tried to be kind.

He snorted derisively at her obvious understatement. "Difficulty? If Cody gets his hands on them, they can't last long in this world. He's probably the most well-known human in pet heaven and he's only five years old!"

Sasha glared at her visitor.

"What your son needs, Reverend Windsor, is something to take his mind off his troubles. A little fun. Some jocund person who can regurgitate his high spirits back to where a five-year-old boy's should be."

"You really do have a thing for all these weird words, don't you? Jocund, indeed." He smiled sadly at her strange choice of words.

But Sasha held his gaze steadily, willing him to accept Cody's distress. And her solution to it. When he inclined his head in a nod, she let her breath out in a whoosh of relief.

"And I suppose you have yourself in mind as this cheerful, animated person who is only too willing to sacrifice herself for the good of our family. To do her Christian duty, in fact.'' His sigh was full of long-suffering patience.

She nodded slowly, keeping her gaze fixed on him. ''Well, I don't know about sacrifice myself. But, yes, I do have a certain perspective that you seem to lack.''

He muttered something disparaging.

''I beg your pardon?''

''I said there's always one. At least.'' His voice was full of bitterness.

She frowned. ''One what?''

He glared at her angrily.

''One do-gooder busybody who thinks she knows exactly what my son and I need in our lives. And she usually volunteers herself as that solution.'' He paused to stare at her expectantly. When it became obvious to him that she had no idea as to the direction of his thoughts, Jacob Windsor clarified matters in a cold, mocking tone. ''As Cody's new mother. And my wife.''

Sasha couldn't help it, her eyebrows rose to their full height as her eyes widened in shock at his words.

''I'm not proposing anything of the sort,'' she informed him in a squeaky, high-pitched croak that was totally unlike her usually low voice.

''Oh, I'm sure you'll get 'round to proposing fairly soon, Miss Lambert. *They* usually do.''

Fury rose like a red flag in front of a bull and Sasha's reaction was just as quick. She slapped her hands on her hips and surveyed his seated form from her standing position.

''Well, *they* are not me! Of all the patronizing, rude—''

''Forget it,'' he said snidely. ''I've heard it all before. The pie, the little discussion, the motherly concern. They've already been used.''

''Not by me they haven't. I couldn't be bothered.''

The look he favored her with just then sent her temperature soaring several degrees higher. Which was not a good sign, Sasha decided angrily, releasing a breath that puffed the bangs off her forehead.

"Lest you faint away from shock," she said gratingly, struggling to hold on to her temper, "I take great delight in informing you that I have not the least intention of becoming anyone's wife."

"Uh-huh." He nodded smugly. "That's what they all say. At first." He twiddled with the empty pie plate sitting in front of him as he spoke. "I'll give you about five minutes until that tactic changes. The next step is sugar-coated sweetness."

"Ooo-ooh." Sasha's hands formed fists at her sides as she blinked away the red tide of murder from her gaze. She planted herself directly opposite him and leaned in, holding her face mere centimeters from his.

"You may think you're God's gift to this earth, *Reverend*," she rasped. "But let me be the first to have the temerity to suggest that I don't find you so irresistible." She refused to look away from those black depths. "Oh, I'd like to have a child like Cody, make no mistake about that."

"I thought so." The superior look on his face was short-lived as she prepared her ammunition and fired with both barrels.

"But to take you into the bargain seems an awfully high price to pay to be a mother." She stiffened her backbone with barely concealed fury.

"Men!" She spat the word out in disgust. "Let me tell you, buster. Minister or not, I haven't the least interest in you or any others of your kind." Her eyes held his, refusing to look away from their piercing intensity.

"I am a career woman, dedicated to pursuing her own interests and livelihood. I don't need a man to support me or to hold me down or to nurture. I'm fully capable of building my own life." Her teeth hurt from clenching and she eased up on her jaw just a fraction. "If and when I decide to have a child, there are the facilities available. I don't need you to accommodate me there. *Thank you very much!*"

Sasha could feel the heat radiate off her face as she ended the tirade and wondered if she'd been too blunt. At least he had the grace to look embarrassed.

"I'm sorry," he muttered. "I just naturally assumed that you were another—"

She cut him off. "Don't naturally assume anything about me, Mr. Windsor." Sasha tossed her head back angrily. "I like children, a lot. That's all. Period. No strings."

He nodded. "Fine. I understand."

She searched his gray eyes but saw nothing save a faint remnant of suspicion and perhaps a hint of relief.

"What do you suggest I do about Cody, Miss Lambert?"

She sucked in a breath of air and allowed a slight softening to mold the curve of her straight lips. At least he had decided to listen to her opinion concerning Cody's welfare. His gray eyes glinted at her.

"Thank you for your interest in him. And I really do apologize. I guess I was way off base."

"Yes, you were," she agreed pertly. "I am only thinking about Cody."

He nodded gravely. "So am I."

Sasha took that as a green light and proceeded to offer him her advice. "Well, Rev," she began irreverently, enjoying the frown that drew his thick black eyebrows together.

Do him good, she told herself. *Obviously thinks he's hot stuff.*

"The first thing I'd suggest is that you go down to Booker's and see if you can find another goldfish to replace Henry. And eventually you're going to have to talk to Cody about this strange idea he has regarding his mother's death."

He nodded, obviously considering her advice.

"I know. I did try, but when we moved and my mother was with us, I thought he'd forget about it. He hasn't had a nightmare for quite a while, but obviously Cody still thinks about Angela. I guess we'll just have to go over the whole thing again." He heaved a sigh that lifted his wide shoulders high. "I'm not anxious to go back to that era."

Sasha watched him covertly.

"You know, part of the problem might be that he's by himself all the time," she suggested softly, and watched as the Reverend Jacob Windsor frowned at her criticism, his back straightening in his chair.

"I spend as much time as I possibly can with my son, Miss Lambert."

Sasha could hear the ice crackling in his voice and decided to drop that aspect. For now. She stood and carried the dishes to the sink, stacking them haphazardly.

"I'm sure you do, Rev. But tonight, I'm going to spend the evening showing Mr. Cody Windsor what a good time is like in Allen's Springs."

Sasha smiled widely. She liked kids, especially their capacity for love. She hadn't had much to do with them lately; not with the store and all. Of course, Allen's Springs usually attracted an older clientele to its rejuvenating mineral waters, although parents and children did come to the lake in the summer. And since she'd moved from Toronto, her siblings had found it expensive to visit.

This was exactly what she needed to get over Dwain, she told herself. Just what she needed to be young and carefree once more, no longer tied to a man who demanded straitlaced perfection and unending cloying devotion in a little town where their every move was relayed back to his fawning mother.

"How?"

She turned in surprise. The Reverend Jacob Windsor stood behind her, a look of expectation on his narrow face.

"Well, let's see…" She paused, thinking madly. "Cody and I are going to go on a picnic."

She grabbed a basket from the closet shelf and considered the contents of her fridge. When a choking sound penetrated her consciousness, she turned to find her guest eyeing the lake trout stretched out across her refrigerator shelf, its glassy eye fixed on them both.

"You're not taking that, are you?" he asked curiously. "I mean, you're not going to serve sushi or something, right?" He frowned down at her, his finger stroking the line of his jutting chin. "You know? Not right after Henry's, er, demise?"

Sasha pointed her chin in the air and ignored his rudeness. She had never even seen sushi!

"*If* you hurry," she intoned snottily, "you might get back with that goldfish in time to go with us." Her eyes flashed indignantly. "Not that I'm inviting you, you understand. I wouldn't want to be accused of pursuing you like some man-hungry female on the make."

She didn't bother to sugar-coat the words although Sasha wondered later if it was exactly the right phrase to use with a minister.

"Yes, ma'am," he quipped, moving toward the door. "I got that message loud and clear."

His eyes glanced across the blur of yellow sticky notes dotting her refrigerator. Each note had a cat prancing across the top and a word scrawled across the bottom. His eyes glimmered with some hidden vestige of humor as he studied their curious poses.

"I think it's only fair to mention, however, that Cody is not an ailurophile. In fact, he's allergic."

He sauntered out the door, a smug smile of superiority curving his lips as Sasha frowned at his retreating back. He was trying to get back at her, make her feel inferior. Well, she'd show him!

She ignored his departure and concentrated on filling her

picnic basket. But, finally, when she could resist no longer, she gave up and dashed out the door after him.

"A what?" she called.

Jake Windsor turned toward her. "An ailurophile. A lover of cats." His gray eyes opened wide, mocking her ignorance. "I was sure you would know that one."

But Sasha was ready for him. "I don't go for bombastic words," she told him saucily. "Too pretentious for a rural area like ours."

With that she marched back into her house to prepare Cody's picnic. And all the while her mind enumerated the indubitable assets of the newest inhabitant to Allen's Springs.

So what if he was tall. Taller than her in fact.

And dark.

And handsome.

She was interested in the son, not the father.

Her mind echoed the unusually descriptive word Jacob Windsor had used earlier.

You're interested in him all right, her subconscious asserted. *But it won't do you any good. He's gun-shy. And you're supposed to be focusing on a different goal.*

Sasha picked up the hamburgers and stored them in a corner of the large basket before checking her appearance in the mirror for the sixth time. Her mouth tipped downward in just the tiniest way as she considered her actions.

Primping! Yuk!

But her mind wouldn't stay off the subject of Jacob Windsor. She'd been truly sad to see Pastor Dan leave after so many years. But now there was Pastor Jacob Windsor. He did present a whole new range of possibilities.

Of course, they have nothing to do with the fact that he's young and good-looking and four whole inches taller than me, she assured her subconscious in a severe tone. *Nothing at all!*

She knew she lied.

Chapter Two

"Amen." Cody's loud voice reverberated through the solemn silence of the woods later that afternoon.

Jake watched as Sasha Lambert leaned down to drop a few handfuls of the rich dark soil onto the tiny box that held his son's dead goldfish.

Cody wasn't quite so dainty and Jake grinned as the little boy heaped up piles of the rich black soil with his bare hands. His pants were dirty and stained and there was a tear in one leg. Again! It was doubtful the shirt would be good for much but the rag basket after today. And Cody's shoes? Well, they could probably be restored to something like their former state.

Somehow.

"We can have the lunch now," his son told them cheerfully. "They always have lunch after funerals. To celebrate the person's life, right, Dad?" He looked from Sasha to his father for confirmation. Jake felt another pair of eyes fasten on him, as well.

"Yes, well, uh, that's right, Cody," he mumbled, and felt embarrassed at the strange look she gave him. She was probably right. A five-almost-six-year-old shouldn't know so much about funerals.

"Sorry, guys." Sasha's cheerful voice broke the silence. "I haven't got a lunch. I've got supper!"

He watched her kneel beside Cody.

"I've got hamburgers and potato salad and pickles and chips and double-chocolate brownies. How about that, sport?"

Cody grinned. "I'm not a sport."

Jake heard him giggle as Sasha tickled him under his chin.

"You're not," she said, pretending astonishment. "I was sure you were a good sport." She rippled her fingers across his stomach and under his arms, drawing out squeals of glee. "Are you sure you're not?"

He watched them cavort in the sun-dappled woods and thought how long it had been since he'd heard his son laugh so readily. Cody seemed to have developed a strong rapport with the owner of the local craft store in a remarkably short time.

Not that she wasn't remarkable herself. Sasha Lambert was every bit as curious as the name she had given to her business. She was tall, stretching to just above his chin, and well rounded in all the right places. He knew that because she was wearing a yellow kind of skirt-shorts thing that showed off those long legs and a scooped-neck knit top that gave him a very good view of all of her assets. He tried to ignore the top's bilious purple color, which bore a significant resemblance to the shade of her unusual furniture.

She was a pretty woman with that black cap of feathery hair cut close to her scalp, cupping the regal lines of her neck. The deep richness of its raven tones highlighted her round, expressive eyes and lent their green hue a clarity that was very effective in raising his temperature when she focused them on him.

He hated that flutter of awareness that tingled low in his stomach. It was, well, a betrayal of Angela somehow. A denial of the place his late wife should hold in his heart. The fact that Angela had died at the lowest point in their marriage was something he refused to think about.

Angela was gone. Why, then, did he feel so guilty? Why couldn't he let her rest in peace?

It was a punishment; he understood that now. He hadn't appreciated his wife's fragility, her inability to handle the myriad problems that came with his job. He'd ignored her complaints and focused solely on the opportunity to get ahead. After all, they would have time later on.

Only they hadn't. And Jake couldn't ever say the words of apology that haunted him yet. He would live with that for the rest of his life. He shoved the thought away.

Despite his best intentions, Jake's eyes persisted in their scrutiny of the vibrant young woman in front of him.

Sasha Lambert was nothing like Angela. She had a wide strong face with prominent cheekbones and a straight nose that tipped at the bottom just a bit. It was her mouth that really told him about her, though.

It curved and slanted and tipped in a thousand different ways when she spoke. Wide and mobile, with flashing white teeth, Jake was fascinated by the many moods delineated on that expressive face. He knew a word that exactly expressed the intangible quality he had seen in Sasha Lambert.

"Gallimaufry." A hodgepodge or mixture of unrelated things. He wondered if he would see that look of delight cross her face again if he told her.

"Can we, Dad?"

Jake awoke from his study to find two pairs of eyes fixed on him. "Uh, I'm not…"

She took pity on him.

"We were just going to go over to the picnic area to get our fire started, Mr. Windsor. Are you coming?"

"Well," he prevaricated, watching her closely. "I'm not sure I'm invited."

She said nothing, waiting for Cody to give the word.

"Sasha always says 'the more the merrier,'" the little boy quoted. "I do, too."

With a whoop of excitement, Cody whirled off after Sasha's dog, tearing wildly through the overhanging boughs.

"'Sasha always says,'?" he questioned softly. "Just how long has Cody been coming into your store, Miss Lambert?"

"About five days, on and off. Long enough to hear me say that, I guess." She kept on walking, glancing placidly around at the trees. "And please call me Sasha. No one in Allen's Springs calls me Miss."

"I'll speak to him," Jake declared out loud. "He shouldn't be bothering you at all, let alone at work. My housekeeper, Mrs. Garner, is supposed to be watching him." His gray eyes searched hers. "And my name is Jake," he told her. "You can forget all that Reverend and Mister stuff."

He frowned, wondering what else he had missed about his son's current life. Hadn't they made any progress after that desolate year when he'd been content to let his parents deal with Cody's and his needs rather than force himself to deal with the raw edges of his own life?

Her voice drew him out of his reflections.

"Actually, I like it when he shows up in the store. I've been thinking of trying a new line of kids' crafts for the children we get in when their parents come to use the spa. Cody's been sort of test marketing things." He watched her eyes close for a moment. "When I was a kid, there were always children around. I miss that."

She glanced fondly at the boy and the dog, hunched together at the bottom of an old oak tree. "He gives Oreo a run for her money, too."

Jake stared. "Oreo?" This was a dog's name?

"Well, she has three chocolate spots and I thought she looked like a cookie when she was a pup." She met his appraising glance with an embarrassed look. "It's probably not appropriate for her breeding title, but who cares." Her shoulders shrugged with indifference.

"Who, indeed," he repeated, mulling over the events of the past hour. What a strange afternoon! But then everything about this woman was unexpected.

"This is the best table in the park," she told him moments later.

Jake watched as she spread a plastic checked cloth over the picnic table and began to unpack the basket he had lugged across the thick grass.

"Aren't you going to start the fire?" she chided, obviously waiting for him to begin.

He glanced up from his scrutiny of her very long, very shapely legs, to find her wide green eyes fixed on him curiously.

"Don't you know how?" she asked kindly.

He felt himself bristle.

"Of course I know how to build a fire. I was the top camper in my Boy Scout troop," he heard himself say smugly.

Oh, for Pete's sake, Windsor, he admonished his overactive ego. It was an innocent offer to help. Don't offend her yet again with your stupid assumptions. As he chopped and split the wood, Jake found himself answering her questions.

"How long have you been in Allen's Springs?"

"Five days, give or take." He grinned. "Cody must have been at your place on the first day. I've been so busy unpacking, I guess I haven't paid enough attention." As usual, he added to himself.

She glanced up from unloading the basket.

"Unpacking for so long? I don't think I own enough

possessions to unpack for five days straight. You must have brought a lot of stuff.''

''Yes, there is a lot to deal with. It's all been in storage, you see. Since Angela's death. While we were overseas.'' He said the words without thought.

She had that warm, fuzzy look again. It made him nervous. Jake wasn't sure he had enough strength left in him to fend off another man-hungry female but he sure as heck wasn't ready to fall into the predatory clutches of some lonely woman on the make.

Then again, Sasha had made it perfectly clear that she wasn't interested in men, just children. He decided to be cautious. Time would tell if she was merely trying another ploy from the ''single woman syndrome.''

He straightened his spine with determination.

''What was it like?'' The words were soft and dreamy, barely audible above Cody's roughhousing with Oreo.

Jake frowned. ''What was what like?''

''Overseas?''

He had to grin at his own foolishness. Sasha Lambert wasn't a repressed spinster, she was a repressed traveler! He felt even sillier now.

''Well, I spent quite a lot of time at Oxford, actually. The past two years I've been working on a dissertation for my doctoral thesis. It was a much slower pace than I'd been used to. The life we led in Toronto wasn't conducive to a lot of internal meditation.''

''England,'' he heard her breathe. ''I've always wanted to go there. Everything looks so lush and green in pictures people bring back.''

Jake watched her wide green eyes sparkle with enthusiasm as she stared, totally unfocused, at her own verdant surroundings.

''Tower Bridge, the Crown Jewels. Oh,'' she gasped as another thought struck. ''Did you see Windsor Castle?''

He nodded. It was refreshing to see such excitement.

Even Cody hadn't been this enthused by their numerous sight-seeing excursions, and it was supposed to have been his holiday!

"All of it that I could," he told her. Jake studied her in the bright sunlit glade.

"I guess you would. How does it feel to have your own castle?" Sasha giggled, her jade eyes twinkling at some inner joke.

He cast her a frowning look.

"You know, Windsor Castle—Jacob Windsor?"

He grinned.

"Oh, I don't go back much now," he told her in the Queen's good English. "Too many drafts, you know. Have you traveled much?" Jake studied her smiling face with interest.

Sasha shook her dark head sadly.

"No. I was to have gone to Hawaii last winter but Dwain…" She let the words trail away, leaving him more curious than ever about her and the man she'd just mentioned. "Well, I think this fire is going to have to burn down some before we can roast anything on it." It was a definite change of subject, but he let her get away with it.

Jake watched her slide gently to the grass, her long legs curled beneath her. Legs like that should be covered, he told himself, noting their smooth curves with growing interest. He quelled that inner spark of awareness and seated himself opposite her, keeping a watchful eye on Cody.

"Now you know about me," he said. "Let's hear about you."

She shrugged her shoulders.

"Nothing much to know. I've lived here for about two years. I like the small community and my business is built around the tourism the mineral springs generates as well as local people who sell their wares to the visitors we get."

Jake noted the glimmer of excitement that darkened her eyes when she spoke of her work. It was a good sign.

Women who were involved in their own lives weren't as likely to interfere in his.

"What did you do before that?" he asked curiously. "Surely you could have traveled then?"

A smile curved her wide mouth, tipping the corners up and showing her even teeth. She shook her dark head.

"Uh-uh. Too busy climbing the corporate ladder. Or trying to."

"So what happened to change that?" Jake found himself studying her. The corporate ladder? Sasha Lambert looked nothing like the hard-nosed businesswomen he associated with corporate ladders.

She tipped her head to one side, nibbling on a fingernail as she considered his question and her answer.

"I hated the anonymity of the city. I moved here to be my own boss. I thought I'd found Mr. Right when I got engaged to Dwain, but my prince turned out to be a frog." She shrugged, grimacing. "A little while ago I suddenly realized that because of him, I wasn't anywhere near achieving the things I really wanted out of life—things that I'd left the city to find."

"Like what?"

"A home of my own. Friends and neighbors who care. Independence. A child." She ticked them off on her fingers.

His ears perked at that as Jake felt all his senses go on red alert. But Sasha wasn't looking at him. She was staring at the patch of grass she had tugged from the ground.

"I guess I thought I needed a man to give me all that," she murmured, thinking aloud. "Maybe that's how I got mixed up with Dwain. Everyone sort of paired us off. He is the town's most eligible bachelor, after all!" He heard the self-mockery in her voice and resolved to find out more about the man.

"I knew it couldn't go on. We didn't want the same things. Dwain wasn't interested in family and I want to settle down. When I finally got the courage to have it out with him a couple of months ago, our split caused a nine-day wonder around here. I'm hoping that all that's past now.'' She tipped her head toward him then, chin jutting out defiantly.

''I don't need a man to give my life meaning. And I've realized that Dwain certainly doesn't need *me*. He just needs a dog, a housekeeper and someone to keep him warm.'' She blushed, as if just realizing she was talking to a minister. ''I'm sorry. I shouldn't have said that. Dwain is a nice man, really. I'm just not suited to playing the part of the doting 'little woman of the farm,' I guess.''

She glanced down disparagingly. ''Especially when I'm taller than he is.''

Jake tried to stifle it. He really did.

But the mental picture his mind conjured up of this tall exotic beauty mincing along in the path of some short, toady old farmer was just too much. His shoulders shook with mirth.

''I'm sorry.'' He choked. ''I'm not laughing at you. Really.''

''Yes, you are,'' she returned tartly. Then she grinned. ''But that's okay. Sometimes I have to laugh at me, too.''

He liked her spirit, Jake decided. There were enough poor souls in this world who took things too seriously. He somehow sensed that Sasha Lambert had that irrepressible quality that would help her bounce back from disappointment.

''So exactly what do you do in Bednobs and Broomsticks?'' he asked curiously. ''The name is certainly attention-getting.''

''On purpose. We do everything. I can cater to most events, plus do cake decorating, wedding decorations, veils, bouquets, all kinds of craft supplies and make a whole lot of handmade articles for sale.'' She grinned at him. ''To name a few.''

Jake grinned back. ''But you don't do funerals?''

She took it in stride. "Nope. Sorry."

"And your newest venture is trains?"

"Yes." Her eyes sparkled with animation. "The men here are really getting into the act, especially with all the interest in the restoration of the old train station. They make a great birthday gift." She grinned at him.

"From Cody's reaction, I'll bet the kids like them, too," Jake muttered, watching as her eyes strayed over to the table.

"Is that fire about ready?" she asked. "I'm starved."

"Pretty close," he murmured, offering her a hand up only to find her slim form almost pressed against him when she surged to her feet. He stared into her shimmering green eyes for several moments, sliding his gaze down to note the dewy softness of her lips. Kissable lips. The kind that would taste sweet and haunting, begging him to come back for more.

He wanted to kiss her, to taste the zest and delight she found in life. But the very thought of doing such a thing amazed him. The moments ticked by as he studied the healthy sheen of her skin and the warm coloring that lit her cheeks with an inner light. And even as he stared, Jake felt his own body come alive in a way he hadn't known in months—years.

When Sasha finally moved away, Jake mentally shook himself. He watched her brush at a fly and immediately felt disloyal, remembering how much Angela had detested cooking out of doors. The bugs and dust and smoky odors had set her teeth on edge and yet Sasha seemed perfectly comfortable with all three. As he checked the coals and adjusted the fire until the flames were minimal but gave off a glowing heat, Jake felt the solitude of the green spacious park invade his soul.

He'd missed this, he realized. For the first time in ages, the numbing fog that held him captive seemed to be evaporating, and the colors and smells and vibrancy of life were drawing on his senses. Maybe it was time he got back into living.

"Fire's about right, I'd say. I'll get Cody if you want to start the burgers." He had only taken a few steps when she muttered something. "I beg your pardon?" Jake searched her gleaming eyes.

"I said, that's all I am to you—a cook? Talk about preconceived notions! How like a male chauvinist!"

He grinned appreciatively.

"I'm not quite that puerile," he chided and stalked away, enjoying the frown on her face. Halfway across the lawn he relented and turned back, ready to explain, but she forestalled him.

"No," she agreed, staring at her hands and speaking so softly Jake barely heard the words. "I think you're far beyond the childish stage. And that has probably discomfited more than a few women." He barely heard the last few whispered words. "Me, included."

As he strode over the uneven terrain, Jake grinned to himself. There was something about her that made him take himself lightly. He liked that. He'd been too serious for far too long.

But that's all it was, he told the clear blue sky. Just someone to talk to and maybe a friend for Cody. He didn't want anything else. He couldn't. It was too hard.

They munched on burgers and chips, drank the lemonade and bought an ice cream cone from the boy pedaling his little truck through the park.

After that, Cody insisted on a game of catch. Sasha showed them the ducks and rabbits near the pond at the end of the park and they fed the animals the scant remains of their supper. It was an idyllic evening that Sasha allowed herself to thoroughly enjoy.

As she packed everything up, Cody's tired voice penetrated her musings.

"We're just like a real family, Dad," he murmured,

snuggling his head against his father's broad shoulder as the sunlight waned and darkness loomed among the tall pines.

"A mom and a dad and a kid."

Sasha felt his fist tugging her heartstrings once more. It was uncanny the way the child got to her this way. Just a few words and she was ready to forfeit her hard-won independence for the sake of a motherless little boy.

"It was fun, son," she heard Jacob say. "But now I think we'd better get you into bed. Tomorrow's Sunday and I've got a bit of work to do on my sermon yet."

"Oh, please," Sasha murmured, anxious not to waylay him. "Go ahead home. I'll take the shortcut to my place. There's no need for you to walk me there."

His gray eyes were clear and focused as he met her gaze.

"It's not a problem," he said. "Cody and I will see you home first."

She read the underlying words with no difficulty. And knew why he didn't want to say them. It would be tantamount to admitting they'd had a date if he said he never let a woman walk home alone. And the last thing Jacob Windsor intended was to have her—or anyone else—think that he wanted a woman in his life.

"Show me the shortcut," was all he said.

So she did. And ten minutes later they were at the side door of her business-cum-home.

"Thanks for a lovely time," she murmured, unwilling to wake the drowsy child.

"We should be thanking you," he returned. "I'll try to ensure that Cody doesn't make a nuisance of himself anymore."

She knew it was pointless to tell him that she enjoyed the energetic little boy. Jacob Windsor would only see it as her attempt to inveigle herself into his good graces.

Instead Sasha smiled and eased in through the door with her basket, murmuring a soft good-night.

It didn't take long to get ready for bed and she decided to sit on the patio for a few moments in the dark. Sasha enjoyed the solitude. It was especially gratifying to sit outside tonight relaxing and thinking of the past few hours.

Thanks, Lord, for letting me see that there are still some real men in the world.

Sasha grinned to herself.

Even if they're not for me. That sounded childish.

Not that I need one. Defiant. That was better.

Except to have a child with. She got up and climbed the stairs to bed. It was the same old circuitous argument that led nowhere and answered none of her questions.

Biological clock or not, she still ached with this incredible longing to have her own child, to create a family circle of her very own. Why would she feel this way if God intended her to remain single?

There was no answer.

Sunday morning dawned bright and clear, which seemed to account for the large crowd at church. That and the fact that it was the first Sunday for the new minister. Sasha glanced around the small sanctuary and noticed the wealth of females in attendance.

A small grin twitched at the side of her lips. Let's see you wiggle out of this one, Reverend Windsor, she snickered as she ticked off the possible contenders.

Mrs. Garner was old enough to be his mother, but she sat there, front and center, decked out in her Sunday-go-to-meeting hat and a brand-new dress. Sasha made a mental note to check whether the woman had shed her customary brown support hose for the occasion. Cody sat by the woman's side, eagerly gazing 'round the small church.

Flora Brown, the church secretary, was also an older single woman. Today her mousey dry hair was ruffled into a new style that took years off her plain face. And she was not wearing black!

Maudie Roach, as I live and breathe. Sasha barely stifled the tickle of laughter that begged release as the town's most eligible female sauntered suggestively down the aisle and placed herself in the center seat, second row. Her shapely figure was displayed to perfection in the fitted white silk suit she wore. A thigh-high slit in the skirt showed off her slim legs and dainty toes in sandals with four-inch heels.

For one green moment Sasha allowed jealousy to invade her. Just once she'd like to be short enough to be able to wear heels that endowed her with a regal grace and elegance instead of these plain flatties that minimized her five-foot-eleven-something stature.

And next to the expensive cut of Maudie's outfit, Sasha's own floral sundress looked home-made. Which it was, she mocked herself gently. She'd given up buying haute couture outfits when she'd moved to Allen's Springs to become independent. *A decision which I do not regret,* she assured herself sternly.

"Morning, Vera."

Looking frazzled and hot, Mrs. Bratley slipped onto the empty seat beside her, fingers clenched around the wriggling arm of her five-year-old son Bobby.

Sasha smiled sympathetically.

"Having a tough day?" she murmured as she watched the town brat snitch a soda cracker from the baby behind them.

"Just the usual." Vera sighed. "Bobby didn't want to come to church today. Hector's gone fishing, you see."

Sasha nodded. She knew exactly how Bobby felt. There had been times in her life when she would have far preferred to worship God in the cool stillness of the river rather than the stuffy confines of First Avenue Church.

While his mother leafed through the bulletin, Sasha slipped the child a mint, which he promptly chewed while holding his hand out for a second.

"Sorry," she whispered. "That's all I have."

He went for her handbag, but Sasha slipped it to the other side just as the Reverend Jacob Windsor moved behind the pulpit.

It wasn't a long service. The hymns were familiar upbeat ones that encouraged and uplifted the spirit. Maudie favored them with a solo that had the rafters resounding with pure, clear contralto tones that Sasha refused to allow herself to envy.

But the message... Now that was something else.

He started off well, Sasha decided.

"Cody and I would like to thank each of you for your kind welcome to Allen's Springs. We are looking forward to getting to know all of you much better in the weeks and months ahead."

And then came the warning.

"Although my wife has passed away, Cody and I are very happy together. We have many fond memories that we share when we're feeling low. And so, while I appreciate the numerous invitations you've so graciously extended, we must have time to find our place together in this community."

It was well said, she'd give him that. But the intent was still the same.

Back off.

There were more words along the same lines, but Sasha tuned the rest out as she surveyed the crowd for reactions.

Mrs. Garner was studying her gloves as if they were covered with some distasteful substance while Flora sat stiffly facing the front. Sasha couldn't detect even the twitch of muscles in the harsh profile view. Two teenage girls were giggling and whispering to each other as they cast wide-eyed soulful eyes at Jacob.

But it was Maudie who made her teeth clench.

Gorgeous, self-aware Maudie, who leaned back in her seat comfortably. A predatory look that Sasha had seen numerous times curved the full red lips. In a movement as old as time, Maudie flicked back the silver-gilt curls with a careless twitch of her neck, her eyes studying the man in front of them all.

She's gonna go for him, Sasha's subconscious whispered. *She's loaded for bear.*

The words rattled around and around her brain as the pastor pronounced the benediction. They ate away at her as she bid her friends and neighbors good morning. They nagged her conscience as she shook Reverend Windsor's hand and facetiously thanked him for the "enlightening" sermon.

They hissed at her as she watched Dwain amble over to Maudie, trying desperately to get the other woman's attention.

Warn him. Tell Jake what to expect.

"Lovely job of the bulletin, Flora. I really like those cartoons on the back."

Tell him to be careful. If she gets her hooks in, he'll wonder what hit him.

"Cody! It's nice to see you again. I do like that shirt."

Do you want Maudie Roach to become that child's mother?

"Stop it," she snapped, causing old Mr. Abernathy to pull his hand away abruptly.

"I'm sorry," she apologized, red-faced. "I was thinking of something else." She watched him walk away with a frown.

"Home, I need to go home. Get out of this sun." Sasha hoped no one would notice she was talking to herself.

"Exactly what I was thinking." Maudie stood smiling artlessly down at her, Pastor Jacob directly behind holding the handle of her white parasol with two fingers. "You bigger women always seem to have trouble with the heat."

"Bigger women" indeed!

It was a direct slam that hit home painfully since Sasha was only too conscious of her own overly large frame when measured against the other woman's petite size. Sasha held her hands at her side, curved her nails down and forced her lips to smile.

"Oh, you don't worry about me, Maudie. I'm not the one who needs a parasol. Actually, I'm quite strong. I don't need a man to protect me from the elements."

The woman looked like a cat, Sasha decided. A very contented cat as she curled her arm into the minister's muscled black-robed arm.

"Oh, I just love having a big strong man around. It's so refreshing to be taken care of."

You and Scarlett O'Hara, Sasha thought, turning away. It was disgusting. She strode down the road, heading for home like a scared rabbit. Enough was enough!

She stripped the dress off in her bedroom and slid on a cool cotton romper that allowed the air to caress her heated skin.

"Bigger woman, indeed," she muttered, assembling a sandwich for herself from the assortment of cold cuts and the garlicy dill pickles she loved. She was proud of her height and her well-endowed figure. She was!

Sasha refused to admit that she had donned the outfit in the hopes that a certain man and his son would stop by. She tried to remember all the confident, self-reliant messages she had learned while disengaging herself from a dependent relationship with Dwain.

I am strong...I am invincible.

Sasha grinned as the old Helen Reddy tune whirled through her head. She should have roared at Maudie. It would have been preferable to all the purring Maudie had aimed at the congregation's new spiritual leader.

The lazy June afternoon stretched before her, hot and empty. Since she didn't have to be in the store and none of the six crafts she currently had on the go appealed right now, Sasha decided to spend the next few hours in pure, self-indulgent decadence.

Twenty minutes later she was sprawled on a blanket in the backyard with a frosty glass of lemonade, a bowl of fudge-almond ice cream and a romantic novel to wile away her time sunbathing.

It was a good book and she was well into the third chapter before the noise penetrated. Kind of a tapping. Cody Windsor stood outside her gate, tears pouring down his round cheeks.

"Why, Cody! What's the matter? Are you hurt?"

She squatted, getting on his eye level while her fingers moved briskly over his arms and legs. Nothing seemed broken but his face was a mess of dirt, grass and scratches.

He shook his head, dislodging pieces of leaf from his dark head with the motion. One fat tear dribbled down his face to plop on his filthy shirt, cutting a path through the grime that covered his freckled face.

"Well, what then? Are you sick?" She led him through the gate and onto her blanket. He had stopped that awful sobbing now. But every so often a hiccup slipped out. The sound tugged at her heart. "Cody, what's the matter?"

His big brown eyes stared up at her, lashes slowly blinking.

"That boy, that bad boy. He beated me up. He said I was a baby."

Sasha felt her heart sink. Bobby, it had to be. He had learned might was right from his older brothers. Probably in order to survive.

Carefully she dabbed at the child's scraped knees with her towel, dampened from the outside tap.

"Does your dad know where you are?"

Tears started again as Cody shook his head.

"He's at home. With a lady. He promised to take me fishing and then that lady came. I went for a walk."

She knew exactly who "that lady" referred to. Why couldn't Maudie have butted out, just for once? Sasha fumed. Resolve straightened her backbone.

Well, Cody was going to go fishing whether Maudie Roach liked it or not. And he was going to go with his father.

"Stay here," she told him firmly. "You can have a drink of my lemonade while you wait. I'll be right back." And marching into the house, Sasha grabbed the phone. "We'll see who's a 'big' woman," she muttered, the words still stinging.

"Jake Windsor." He answered in a harried voice, as if he were distracted.

"Reverend Windsor, this is Sasha Lambert. Cody is here and he needs you." She listened to his worried questions. "No, he's fine. Or he will be. Just get over here."

"Is it that much of an emergency?" he asked softly, obviously trying to keep the conversation from big ears, Sasha decided.

"I think it is," she murmured. "When you're five and your dad promises to take you fishing, that's pretty important."

She could hear the smile in his voice.

"Yes, I think it is, too. I'll be there in five minutes."

"Oh, and Reverend?"

"Yes?" He sounded worried. Good.

"If you spot Bobby Bratley on your way, bring him along, will you? I think he and Cody need to have a discussion."

There was a long pause before he answered.

"Yes. All right."

Chapter Three

"Where is he?"

Jacob Windsor sounded agitated. Sasha watched him rake a hand through his dark shaggy hair. He was casually dressed in a pair of ragged jeans and an old T-shirt that emphasized the powerful muscles beneath.

"Did you find Bobby?" Sasha asked.

"Nowhere to be seen." He shook his dark head. "Why did you want him?" The gray eyes curiously surveyed her swim-suited figure.

Sasha suddenly wished she had taken the time to pull on a coverup. But what with mopping up Cody's injuries and trying to stop the tears, there hadn't been time. She remembered her own pep talk and stood proudly in front of him.

"Bobby and Cody had a little contretemps. Cody came out with cuts and bruises. And wounded pride." She surveyed him angrily. "I thought you didn't want any *woman* intruding on your lives. Why then would you cancel a very special date with your son to entertain one?"

"I didn't invite that...barracuda," he retorted angrily. "She breezed in, complete with a four-course meal, and proceeded to organize us into her version of domestic bliss.'' His head shook with disgust. ''Apparently there is a lot about the word 'no' that Miss Reach doesn't understand.''

Sasha couldn't help it. She had to laugh.

''Her name is Roach. And it's not totally her fault, you know.'' She giggled. ''No one has ever said it to her before.''

''I did. Several times. I don't think she'll make that mistake again.'' His gray eyes glinted silver in the strong afternoon sun when he grinned. ''She made another error when she called you big,'' he stated frankly, his eyes assessing her shape once more, gleaming as they slipped over her well-rounded hips, narrow waist and full bust. They came to rest on the bit of cleavage that showed above her aqua maillot. ''You're very, er, well suited to a bathing suit.''

Sasha flushed. ''Don't start that garbage,'' she muttered, flushing darkly as she chanced a look up from between her lashes. ''Or I'll think you have some hidden agenda— maybe looking for a wife.''

His eyes widened in surprise before he grinned, unabashed. ''Touché. Although why people always think ministers are blind to everything around them, I don't know. We're just as able to appreciate the good things in life as any other man, you know.'' He grinned cheekily. ''Can I see Cody now?''

She stood to the side and let him pass before moving into the house to race upstairs, grab a sundress and tug it on. When she returned outside, she heard Cody complaining to his father.

''Well, I think she was rude not to wait until we asked her if she wanted to stay for dinner. You always tell me to wait till I'm asked. She didn't.'' Cody sniffed self-righteously. ''She ruined our plans.''

Sasha watched Jake scoop the little boy onto his lap.

"Well, just because someone else is rude doesn't mean we have to be, too. Besides, I'm not sure there is any place to fish around here. Everything seems to be saltwater."

"Yes, there is, Reverend Windsor," Sasha interrupted, handing him a glass of lemonade and sinking onto the opposite end of the blanket. "There is a place called Fincher's Creek. You can catch fish to your heart's desire there."

"Can we go, Dad? Can we?" Cody's face brightened as if it were Christmas morning.

The thin, craggy face glanced from his son to Sasha. "I don't know the way," he said simply.

"Sasha can show us," Cody promised. His brown eyes glowed. "And then, when we catch all the fish, she could cook them for us."

Jake grinned at her, a lock of inky-black hair falling across one black eyebrow as he shrugged his broadly muscled shoulders.

"That's his own chauvinism showing through," he told her, tongue-in-cheek. "I didn't teach him a thing."

"Probably absorbed it in utero," she muttered, and then sucked in a breath. What an incredibly stupid thing to say! The last thing Jake Windsor needed was to be reminded of all he had lost. But when Sasha looked up at him, he was laughing. He seemed totally unaware of her faux pas.

"Could be," he agreed, his gaze fixed on his son chasing the dog. "Angela was not what you would call liberated." He stood suddenly, as if only then realizing that he was discussing his dead wife with a virtual stranger.

"I suppose we'd better get going if we intend to fish," he murmured.

"Just let me get some jeans on and I'll show you the way." She turned to go and then turned back thoughtfully. "Doesn't Cody have anything else to wear but those dress clothes? He'll get pretty dirty out there and his fancy duds could get ruined."

"Could get ruined?" Jake snorted. "They look that way

right now. But I get your point. I'll have to get him some more American-style clothing.'' His brow furrowed as he tried to explain.

''They wore uniforms, you see. In England, I mean. They seemed appropriate for him then. And he never got *them* so dirty.''

''At the risk of sounding like a female chauvinist, what can I say? He's a boy, isn't he?'' Sasha grinned, raising her palms heavenward. ''And, Lord knows, boys are messy.''

His chuckles followed her into the house where she tugged on a white cotton shirt and denims. With her feet tied into a pair of ratty old jogging shoes, she was ready to go.

She thought for a moment before allowing her fingers to snitch a few cans of pop and several chocolate bars from the fridge. She placed them carefully in a small cooler bag along with a plastic container for any fish they caught and a filleting knife. It was self-preservation, she told that snickering little voice inside. She hated cleaning fish.

''Ready,'' she called, slamming the door closed. ''Let's hit Fincher's and you guys can strut your stuff.'' She left them there, daring each other to catch the largest fish. ''I'll see you at my place when you've caught your limit,'' she said.

His head jerked around to stare at her, mere inches away from hers as he knelt to help Cody with his rod. She hadn't realized how close they were and when he bent forward, his mouth was so near, she could breathe in the spicy scent of his breath and knew Maudie had served him her usual barbecue ribs.

Sasha stepped back quickly, avoiding his touch. It was the second time she'd felt these sparks of electricity jump across the air between them. For the first time in her life, Sasha was totally aware of her own femininity.

"Oh, but don't you want to…" His eyes were wary as they watched her move away.

She shook her head. "Uh, no. Thanks. I've gotta work on the books today." Before he could say any more or see the blush of awareness that covered her face, she moved off down the road.

In fact, Sasha did very little book work that day. She tidied up her living quarters a little, fiddled with her hair and baked a blueberry pie, but she never actually got down to opening even one ledger.

When her friend Deidre stopped by at four, Sasha barely stemmed the tide of frustration that threatened to overcome her. She wanted the three of them to have some time together. Selfishly, she hoped Deidre wouldn't stay.

"Are you busy?" Deidre asked, her long brown hair swinging over one bare shoulder. "I can always come back later."

"No!" Sasha swallowed and lowered her voice, infusing it with feigned placidity. She hoped. "No, I'm not busy at all right now. Come on in, or rather, let's go sit on the patio. It's too hot in here." Sasha flicked the air-conditioner a notch higher before moving toward the door.

"You're baking? Today?" Deidre quirked one eyebrow at the cooling pie. Her glance at the thermometer hanging outside the kitchen door suggested Sasha was crazy. But Deidre didn't say another word, merely accepted a can of cola with alacrity and sank down onto one of the lawn chairs as she eyed her friend through narrowed blue eyes. "Okay, Sash, what gives?"

There wasn't any point in prevaricating. Deidre Lang didn't know the meaning of the word "quit" and she would keep digging until she got what she wanted.

"Cody Windsor and his dad are coming here once they've caught their limit at Fincher's. I promised I would fry the fish." She met Deidre's sneering look with her chin thrust forward. "That's all there is to it. Really."

"In a pig's eye!" Deidre sipped her drink thoughtfully. "When a tall, very handsome, unattached man comes on the scene, don't tell me you aren't interested, Sasha, my darlin'. You wouldn't be human!"

Sasha shrugged. "Okay, I'm not human." She picked at the threads of her frayed jean shorts. "You, of all people, know how hard I've worked to make this a success," she said, motioning toward the building behind them. "I've spent eighteen hours a day, every day, working to get Bednobs and Broomsticks off the ground. I almost lost my focus on what I really wanted out of life and why I came here when I began dating Dwain and started living my life on his terms." She shook her dark head. "That's not going to happen again. Not ever."

"But what about getting married, having a child? Don't tell me you've changed your mind about that, as well?"

"Nope." Sasha grinned. "But I don't really want the man part. It's the child I'm after. Sure, I miss having my nieces and nephews to care for, but that's not all of it. You know how much I've always wanted my own family. If I can build up my little nest egg, there's this clinic I can go to and…"

"Artificial insemination?" Deidre stared at her friend. "Is that what you're talking about?"

Sasha nodded. "It's not like you think," she rushed to declare. "The donors are all carefully screened and you choose the features and traits you want for your baby."

Deidre's mouth had dropped to her chest.

"Sasha Lambert! I have never heard anything so, so…clinical in my life. It's…" Her shocked voice died away.

"It's the only way for me to have a child, Didi. I'm twenty-eight. I live out here in the boonies. How am I going to meet a man, fall in love and have children when the base population of Allen's Springs hasn't changed in ten years?" She stared off into the mass of weeds that had overtaken her flower bed. "Not that I would change a thing. The peace and stability are why I moved here in the first place. They are a big part of why I want to raise my child here."

"I know. It's everything you didn't have in your own childhood, right?" Deidre sighed sadly.

A wistful smile tugged at Sasha's full lips. "No, the inner-city ghettos I lived in are nothing like this quiet, peaceful prairie town."

"But you got out, Sash. You made good. You don't have to apologize to anyone."

"True, but at the same time, it's not likely that someone with my background and single to boot would be able to adapt. I have enough money for what I need, but I'm no wealthy socialite. And all the nanny experience in the world isn't going to qualify me for a child. No—" she straightened her shoulders "—artificial insemination is the way it has to be."

She grinned at Deidre. "I've almost got enough saved up. I figure by October I should be able to start the treatments. That means a spring baby. A child that can run and play and feel safe and cared for here. And I'd have friends nearby who would help."

They were both lost in their thoughts until Deidre blurted, "But you've got a perfectly good man coming 'round for supper. Why don't you just vamp the minister?"

"Didi! I've never vamped anyone in my life. Anyhow, Maudie Roach *stopped by* his house today with lunch. If anyone could get him, she could." Sasha grinned smugly. "But, somehow, I don't think vamps are his style!"

"That isn't a vamp," Didi sputtered. "That's a piranha." She made a very unladylike sound.

Sasha smiled as she swallowed the rest of her drink before explaining the futility of making any moves on their new minister.

"And even if I could or wanted to, he's simply not interested. He made that more than clear."

Didi looked interested in this tidbit of information but Sasha forestalled her.

"I'm not saying any more on the subject, Didi. He's not interested in acquiring a new wife and I don't want a husband. Not anymore. I just want a child. Someone of my own to love and care for. I want to be a mom for real just once."

Dwain's condemning voice came back to haunt her. "You never really did look for a partner, Sasha. Not really. You don't want a real man. You want someone to help you get a bunch of kids for that dream you have of yourself as the mother of a brood of little angels. What we're really talking about here is a sperm donor."

It wasn't true. Not completely. Sasha had spent a long time searching for Mr. Right. For a while she'd tricked herself into believing Dwain was *the* one. She had hoped she could forget about his faults, his mother and his height and settle down with him. But since Dwain had failed the children test, Mr. Right had never shown up. He wasn't likely to walk in now.

She had to get on with her life. If that meant being a little unconventional, so be it! She had been an oddball for a long time now. The round peg that wouldn't fit the square hole. The oldest in the family and the only one still unmarried. Twenty-eight was not the time to change her personality. Okay, so she might not be able to find Mr. Right, but she could be a mother. With a little help.

"Come on," she teased her friend, tugging her from her comfortable chair. "You can help me clean the flower bed as repayment for that drink."

And Deidre, being the friend she was, cheerfully knelt and began tugging out huge handfuls of weeds, all the while asking questions at a steady rate. Sasha was relieved the grilling had to stop at last when the fishermen returned with a full bag of cleaned fish.

"Can you stay?" she asked Deidre archly. Her friend had an insatiable appetite where gossip was concerned and Sasha wondered whether it would be an evening of probing that would only embarrass Jake and his son. Sasha puffed out a soft whoosh of relief when Deidre's words came rushing out.

"No, Dennis Fleet and I are going out for dinner. To the Spring's Hotel. You must try their shrimp, Pastor. It's really delicious. Do you like seafood?"

She should have given Deidre more credit, Sasha decided. Her friend wouldn't knowingly hurt a flea.

Jake said little, merely answering her questions and then acknowledging her swift departure with one raised eyebrow. When she was gone he cocked his head to one side and peered down at Sasha.

"She's very, um, inquisitive, isn't she?"

"You haven't seen the half of it," Sasha told him, grinning. "But underneath she's as kind as the day is long."

They had a merry meal of fried fish, fresh lettuce salad, cooked carrots and hot buttered rolls while Cody related their afternoon adventures on the river.

"My dad and I catched the biggest fishes there," he boasted.

"Caught," his father corrected automatically. "And don't rodomontade. It's not polite."

"Huh?" Cody looked blank.

"It means 'to brag or boast.'" Jake's silver eyes glistened across the table at Sasha. "There's another one for your fridge. I looked it up last night."

Not to be outdone, she fixed him with a haughty look.

"It was certainly serendipitous that I met you," she murmured cheekily. "My stock of really bizarre words had gotten pretty low."

He seemed to realize she was making fun of him.

"Well," he smirked gratuitously. "The sagacious among us shall lead them."

Sasha burst out laughing, shaking her head at him. "Reverend! Shame on you!"

His black eyebrows tilted upward at her tone.

"I do believe I read that particular scripture as meek," she teased. "You must have the new *revised* version. But go ahead 'wise man.' Lead on. The sink is over there."

"I ate a passel of food," he grunted. "You can't expect me to get up and work after all that." His eyes twinkled as he moaned sorrowfully, rubbing his stomach. "I mean, I did catch some of those fish. And I cleaned all of them. I may need another piece of pie to give me the energy."

"I can help," Cody volunteered, popping up from his chair. "I know how to clear the table."

"Go to it, sport," Sasha cheered, sipping her coffee gratefully.

"Just take it easy on the dishes, son. We don't want to ruin Sasha's china." Jake's voice was full of gentleness as he watched Cody work.

Sasha burst out laughing. "Puh-leese! I got this strange assortment from Mrs. Archer's yard sale when I first moved here. She needed the money and—" She broke off, embarrassed at having said so much. "Go ahead, Cody. Do your worst."

He was pretty thorough, for a five-year-old. He carefully carried each dish to the counter, then watched as Sasha showed him how to scrape and stack the dishes. Then he insisted on doing it himself. "Dad says we hafta learn to look after ourselves," he told her seriously. "We gotta be indi...indip...we gotta do it ourselves."

She smiled. It seemed she wasn't the only one learning new words. "Independent," she told him softly. "And your dad is right. We all have to learn to do things for ourselves."

She turned to fix Pastor Jacob Windsor with a firm look.

"But just remember that if you do need help, there are people who would be happy to lend a hand. No strings!"

"Point taken, Miss Lambert." He smiled. "And thank you."

"You're welcome." She glanced from one to the other and grinned. "Now, since I cooked and Cody cleared, it's your turn to wash, Rev," she told Jake pertly, glancing down through narrowed eyes. "After all, we wouldn't want to coddle you. Independence comes at a price, you know."

Grudgingly he got to his feet.

"One of these days I'm going to figure out how you always manage to turn the tables on me," he muttered. "And when I do, I'll put the kibosh on your manipulations."

Sasha merely smiled, slipping past him toward the back door.

"Famous last words. I hope we don't all ossify before then."

He stared at her, mouth open in a round *O*. She heard him repeat the word under his breath.

"Ossify—to turn into bone, to become hardened or set in one's ways," she elaborated smugly. "Would you like a sticky note to write it down on?"

"No, thanks." He grinned, assuming the English accent he'd modeled earlier. "But I do think you've committed a ghastly solecism by asking a guest to do the dishes. Simply awful."

Sasha ignored him, heading for her favorite lounge on the patio. "It won't work," she called from her perch outside the door. "I don't embarrass that easily when it comes to free dish-washing. And when you're finished, would you mind feeding Oreo? She loves fish." She heard him muttering.

"Her requests are Brobdingnagian."

Sasha grinned, enjoying their quick repartee. "I read *Gulliver's Travels,*" she hollered. "And maybe my demands are huge. But you can do it. You're an independent man who doesn't need a mere woman to help you out. Good for you!'' A smug smile of satisfaction curved her lips.

Jake muttered something then that Sasha didn't quite catch. Unfortunately his son heard it very clearly.

''Dad!'' Cody's voice was full of reprimand. ''You told me I wasn't supposed to say that word. How come—''

Silence reigned in the kitchen then. A curious secretive silence that boded ill for the future. Sasha snuggled deeper into her chaise longue and enjoyed the tickle of an evening breeze against her skin. She watched as the sunlight began to wane and fireflies came out to snap up unwary mosquitoes. She breathed in the sweet scent of the blooming cherry tree.

And she studiously ignored the hissed whisperings going on inside her home to concentrate on the pleasure of having someone nearby, another human for company.

'''I am woman, hear me roar,''' she hummed loudly and just slightly off key. Let's see what he makes of that, she told her subconscious smugly.

Jake pulled the covers up over his son before sinking onto the edge of Cody's narrow captain's bed.

''Are you gonna listen to my prayers?'' Cody asked, a strange light in his brown eyes.

Jake smiled softly, brushing the shining hair off the boy's freshly scrubbed forehead. ''Don't I always?''

''Yeah. But I'm getting kind of big for that.'' Cody wriggled under the Superman-printed spread, turning his head to stare at the wall. ''Besides,'' he murmured, glancing back, ''sometimes prayers are kinda private. Ya know?''

Angela's big round eyes stared up at him in Cody's little face and Jake felt a fist squeeze his stomach muscles.

Oh, God, let me know the right words to say, he prayed

silently as the weight of single parenthood pressed heavily on his shoulders once more.

"You're absolutely right, Cody. Some prayers are very private. Do you want to say yours alone?" He watched the dark head nod once. "Okay, then. Good night, son."

"Dad?"

"Yes, Cody." Jake watched the little face stare up at him trustingly.

"How did my mom die?"

There it was at last. Stark and bold. A request for the truth where it had always been avoided before. Jake breathed a sigh of relief and sought for the right words. He had no intention of failing his son. Perhaps once Cody knew the truth, they could move ahead.

"Your mom had asthma, son. Sometimes she couldn't get her breath because her lungs sort of closed up. We were on a holiday when you were just a little boy and something in the air started bothering her. She took some of her medicine but it didn't help." Jake swallowed hard, forcing himself to continue. "Her body was tired of fighting and it died. But Mom went up to heaven with God. You know that, don't you?"

Cody nodded, his little face strong and proud.

"And you know that she loved you very much and didn't want to leave you without a mommy?" Cody nodded again. "She didn't ever want to leave her little boy all alone with just his daddy, but she knew that we would take care of each other."

"Is she better now?" Cody's eyes were huge as they stared up at him.

"Yes, Cody. She's very happy in heaven because there isn't any sickness there. But I don't want you to think that she went away because you did something. You didn't. It wasn't anybody's fault. She just couldn't stay with us anymore. Okay?"

Cody nodded. "Sasha said something like that, too," he

murmured. "I thought maybe I did sumthin' God didn't like, but she said it wasn't 'cause I was bad or nothing. She said God wasn't like that."

"No, Cody. Your mom didn't die because of you. That was just a dream you kept having. Do you understand?" Jake watched his son nod sleepily.

Jake kissed the dewy-soft skin and hugged the bony little body close to himself, inhaling the scent of freshly washed boy. Cody hung on fiercely for a few moments and then lay back down, his brown eyes clear as they gazed into Jake's.

"'Night, Dad. Love you."

It was their routine, the constant in Cody's life. It hadn't varied since Angela's death, even though Jake had often treated it as a simple habit to be dispensed with quickly. He regretted that nonchalance. Cody was growing up before his eyes.

"Love you, too, Cody. Sleep tight."

He switched off the bedside lamp and then pulled the door almost closed so that just a sliver of light shone into Cody's room. Seconds later he heard Cody's voice once more.

"It's okay, Dad. I don't need the hall light tonight."

Jake shook his head disbelievingly as he flicked the switch. Cody, who always had to have a light left on, was *asking* him to shut off the lights? Something was very odd.

He walked down the hallway, and then in spite of himself, crept back to stand quietly outside Cody's door. He heard the childish tones clearly through the crack in the door.

"And please God, could you get me Sasha for a mom. I know my dad don't like me to ask him 'bout it, but a guy really needs to have a mom to do things for him."

There was a little hiccup sob then and Jake leaned a bit nearer, ignoring the stab of pain in his heart.

"I know you're taking real good care of my mom up

there and I want to thank you. But I need somebody down here who can help my dad laugh and get me clothes like the other kids and bake triple chocolate chip cookies with nuts, an' kiss me good night.''

A lump formed in Jake's throat that would not be swallowed away. He brushed away the lone tear and took a ragged breath of air as his son continued his heavenly petition.

''But it's not just for eating and stuff. Sasha knows how to have a good time and make people happy. She doesn't act like I'm dumb just 'cause I can't make all my letters. And she hugs me ever so tightly. I like how she smells, too.''

Jake grinned at that. He knew exactly what young Cody meant. He'd been intrigued by Sasha's haunting fragrance himself—feather soft, never overpowering. Deliciously flowery with a hint of spice. Sort of like the woman herself, he decided.

But it seemed that young Mr. Cody Windsor wasn't quite finished.

''An' God, you already know that I really, *really* like worms? Well, guess what? She likes 'em, too! Did you see us dig up a whole bunch this afternoon? We put 'em back, though.''

There was a soft silence as if Cody was trying to remember what else he wanted to say. Then the familiar prayer Jake had heard in some form or other many times took over.

''Bless Shelley and Rolly and George and Gertrude an' Rocket an' Henry. And God bless Daddy most of all and help him get me a mom right away. Amen.''

Jake peered through the crack and, in the wash of moonlight streaming through the window, saw Cody scramble back into bed. Seconds later his son was scooting out, back on his knees again, eyes scrunched up tightly as he spoke softly.

"But I really would like Sasha best of all for my new mom. Amen."

After several minutes Jake moved woodenly, arms and legs stiff with clenching, away from the door and down the hallway to the big family room. Through the windows he could see parents gathering their children together, calling them in from their play. Fathers scooped up bikes and trikes and moved them off the driveways while mothers chided their babes for taking too long to get to sleep.

They were all going through the run-of-the-mill routine that Jake himself had envisioned on the day of Cody's birth. He'd thought then that he and Angela would have forever, time enough to have more children, to watch them grow, to learn to love each other despite the problems they'd had.

In the blink of an eye, everything had changed, shifted, lost its focus when she had died. For a long time he hadn't been able to even think about the future. The most he could do was get through today, to try to forgive himself for the guilt that was his constant companion; the awful knowledge that ate at him knowing his wife had needed him and he hadn't been there for her, never would be now. When tomorrow came, Jake had always figured he'd deal with that then.

But his and Cody's life had changed. After a year under his parents' care, they had gone on alone and somehow he'd found a way to face each day. Head office had been right. England had helped him survive some of the stigma of a church split, had given him a perspective of sorts.

But it could never erase the guilt he still carried. He hadn't been able to help his congregation deal with their struggles any more than he'd helped his wife deal with hers. He wasn't strong and capable. He certainly didn't have the answers everyone expected. He was just as confused and mixed up as his parishioners. How had he expected to help them overcome the distrust and dissension that had crowded into their midst when he couldn't sort out his own life?

Now he remembered Angela with sadness and not a little pain. She'd had no idea of the life they would lead, of the demands the congregation would make on their time together. Neither had he. But their life together was in the past. And it didn't really matter how much he wanted to change things for his son, to make it different. He couldn't marry anyone. For if there was one thing Jake was certain of, it was that he could never go through the agony of losing someone again.

He grimaced. Sasha had been right. He was a minister. He was supposed to have all the right words when someone died. He was supposed to know how to get past all this. He had preached for years that God forgave humans for their weaknesses. And yet here he was, three years later, still haunted by the loss of his wife and his part in her unhappiness.

"Your church has survived," the district superintendent had written him in Oxford. "It is true that they are separated, but both are busy doing the work of the Lord and we must be thankful for that. Also, please be assured that they bear you no ill will."

Jake had smiled grimly at that. They had more mercy than he had on himself. He still blamed his own lack of understanding for failing them all.

Jake straightened his shoulders, drawing strength into himself as he turned toward the study. Perhaps he hadn't failed God, but he knew without a doubt that he had failed Angela miserably, just as he'd undoubtedly fail if he was stupid enough to try marriage again. In his mind, he turned off the softly pleading words his son had just uttered.

He'd talk to Cody tomorrow, he promised himself. He'd explain that there was just going to be the two of them from now on. He'd tell his son that Sasha Lambert was Cody's special friend but that she couldn't be his mother.

Jake closed his eyes against the thought, leaning back to stretch full-length on the recliner Angela had given him for their first wedding anniversary. He'd felt so strong and capable then, so ready to take on the world. Anxious to climb the ranks, with Angela by his side, and show himself competent and proficient in his work. He'd been so certain in those early days that she would find her place as his helpmate and as a sounding board for the congregation. How he had misjudged her!

Angela had tried; he knew that. She had sat up nights alone with Cody, nursing their baby through months of colic while he'd been away. Over and over she had forgiven him for forgetting important dates and dinners she'd arranged. And when the bickering and infighting had begun, she'd fought desperately to stay neutral while Jake made ever more demands on her. In the end, she'd used the only weapon she had—her illness—to make him listen. By then it was too late. Angela had grown too ill to shake it off.

Now he felt nothing, shut off, afraid to let life fill him with love again. He couldn't let someone—Sasha—get that close again. Not anymore. He couldn't deal with the expectations and the regrets she would have. Not if it meant he would have to go through this hell again. Not when he was just managing to get his life back together for the first time in almost three years. And he wouldn't subject Cody to it, either. Not for anything.

Sasha's not like Angela, his subconscious chided him. *She has her own life, her own plans. She's strong and independent.*

Jake let his mind dwell on the tall, slim, dark-haired woman for a few moments before shoving the thought away. No, it was impossible. She wouldn't have any more idea than Angela had how demanding his career could be. And like Angela, it would wear on her, drag her down, make her resent him and his work. He wouldn't—

couldn't—go through the agony of watching Sasha's lively jade eyes grow dull and listless because of him.

The words slipped into his tired brain of their own accord.

Not even to give your son the one thing he wanted most in this world? Not even to get Cody a mother?

He shook his head firmly. *No!*

Not even for that.

Chapter Four

"Agatha, don't you think Darla's going overboard just a bit with this wedding?" Sasha asked softly. She watched the concern etch the older woman's features.

"Well, I did think the rotating wedding cake was a bit much but you managed that beautifully." Mrs. McMurtry smiled sweetly as she twisted her plump pink hands in her lap. "Besides, Darla says all the city weddings are having these party favors as well as the wedding cake and I do want everything to go well."

"I know." Sasha frowned skeptically. "And I can price these out, of course, but I really think I should talk to Darla. Perhaps she's forgotten some of the other things she's already ordered."

Privately, Sasha thought the McMurtrys's spoiled brat had already been indulged to the max. Her parents were going broke providing Darla with every single wedding frippery she demanded. Maybe she could make the girl see the light where her mother had failed.

"What is her number in Billings, Agatha?"

Sasha scribbled down the information rapidly and decided she would have a one-to-one chat with the bride-to-be. It would be hard enough to carry off this monstrously complicated wedding and reception in the Allen's Springs town hall, never mind the distribution of prewedding favors to the guests' hotel rooms, the delivery of chocolates on pillows at night and the release of five hundred helium balloons to be set free in the local park when the bride threw her bouquet.

She double-checked the items already in stock for Darla's fantastic showpiece to make sure everything was well in hand.

"We've got it all covered, Agatha." Privately Sasha muttered, Unless that girl comes up with yet another outrageous plan.

"It's ridiculous," she groaned to Didi later that morning. "Darla's set on this outlandishly expensive wedding. She'll spend enough for a down payment on a house, for Pete's sake!"

Didi stared as a whistle formed on her lips. "That much?"

"The bridal dress alone is way over two thousand. Add on flowers and gifts for six bridesmaids and groomsmen, four flower girls, various escorts and a catered meal…and you get the idea. Agatha said they're taking out a loan against the farm to cover it." Sasha shook her dark head. "What I want to know is who gets that ostentatious cake when all's said and done. It's not as if you can eat the thing. I had to special order it just to make sure we'd get the thing in time."

She held up one hand as Didi's mouth fell open.

"And before you ask, yes, she has ordered three hundred pieces of wedding fruitcake that are being professionally wrapped and boxed in Billings."

"Three hundred?" Deidre's voice was a squeak. "She's invited *three hundred* people to a wedding in Allen's

Springs?'' The blue eyes were wide open. ''She's really putting on the dog.''

''And breaking her parents in the process. The girl has a really good job in the city. I don't understand how she can't pay for any of this herself.'' Sasha reached across to pick up the phone.

''Bednobs and Broomsticks,'' she recited automatically. For a while she thought no one was there but after several moments Jake Windsor's low tones rumbled across the lines.

''It seems so strange to hear that.''

''Fine thank you. And you?'' It came out spontaneously, without a second thought, and Sasha flushed as he laughed.

''Okay. Right down to business.'' He cleared his throat. ''Actually, I'm calling about a wedding I've been asked to perform this afternoon. It's a rush thing, but the couple asked that we hire someone to decorate the church and the hall for them. They thought about this much to cover the church and hall decorations.'' He named a hefty figure. ''They want something elegant and not overdone. Lots of flowers.''

Sasha whistled. Her eyebrows lifted as she considered his words.

''A wedding?'' Her brow furrowed in thought. She hadn't heard of anyone in the small community getting married.

He waited patiently and when she didn't respond, slowly repeated the information. ''Well? Can you do it?''

''Of course.'' Sasha answered smartly. Why look a gift horse in the mouth? ''Any specific colors in mind?''

Jake's dry tones rumbled in her ear.

''Carte blanche. They're here on vacation. Older couple—mid-forties. Wedding's in the church at five. Can you be ready by then?''

Sasha considered the information and checked her schedule. Didi was covering this afternoon anyway. Why not?

"Sure," she told him airily. "Not a problem. I'll be over in twenty minutes." She relayed it all to Didi while she packed the fluffy ivory tulle bows with their center arrangements of tiny silk irises.

"Aren't these for Darla's wedding?" Didi asked curiously, eyeing the box of stuff she was lugging to the car with suspicion.

"Yep." Sasha nodded, ticking off items on her mental list. "But if I know Darla McMurtry, she'll change her mind seven times before September. This way I can use them, charge for them and when Darling Darla doesn't want to use them, Mrs. McMurtry won't be out a cent." She slammed the door on her wagon and puffed out a sigh, ruffling the bangs on her forehead.

"I don't know when I'll be back," she told her friend. "If I'm not here, go ahead and close at five-thirty." She climbed into the loaded car and then stuck her head back out.

"Anything else I can do?" Deidre asked.

"Phone Mrs. Bratley and ask her to cut whatever flowers she can spare. Price isn't a problem. I'll pick them up in ten minutes. Thanks, Didi."

Two hours later Sasha stood back to admire her handiwork. The church looked coolly elegant with banks of royal blue silk flowers on either side of the wide stairs. A huge arrangement of fresh pansies, asters, lilies and irises sat on the platform, weaving a sweet pungent fragrance throughout the small sanctuary. Alternating royal blue and white candles stood ready to light and the big fluffy bows were attached to the pews.

"Now for the hall," she muttered, tugging the empty boxes behind her.

"I can help you with that." It was Jake, tall and lean, gazing around from the entry. "Although by the looks of it, you don't need any help at all. This is very attractive."

She curtsied. "Thank you, sir." She eyed his mangled

jeans and shabby shirt with a prejudiced eye. "Shouldn't you be changing for the ceremony?" she asked, wondering about his offer of help.

There was no way she wanted to overstep his boldly drawn line that clearly stated No Trespassing. He'd made it very obvious that he preferred solitude to the company of women. Especially single women.

"Lots of time yet." His gray eyes studied her red face and the perspiration she felt gathering on her forehead. "Come on," he motioned. "I'll spring for a soda. I've got some next door."

Sasha trailed along, wondering if he realized that he was inviting a single woman into his home unescorted. A single woman who wanted a child of her own, nonetheless.

"Aren't you afraid I'll compromise you or something," she half teased, studying his face as they ambled across the church lawn. "I mean, I know how much you and Cody need to be alone together, to bond in this new setting."

He grimaced. "Ouch! I guess I did lay it on a little thick. Don't worry, Flora's already chewed me out for that. Let's just say I've had some bad experiences in the past year which I do not wish to repeat."

The manse was a lovely split level that Sasha had secretly admired for years. It looked a little sparse at the moment, but she could visualize an old leather wing-backed chair in front of the fireplace and Cody curled up on the floor beside it, playing with his dog. Which just happened to look remarkably like Oreo.

Stop that, she ordered her brain.

"Come on into the kitchen," Jake urged her. "Mrs. Garner made Cody some cupcakes this morning. Have one." He thrust a hand out toward the happy-faced cakes lined up on the counter.

"No, thanks. I can't afford to eat another thing today."

"Big lunch date?" he asked, one black eyebrow raised inquiringly.

Sasha shook her head, pressing the chilled can against her forehead as she followed him down several stairs to the family room on the next level. It was cooler there and she accepted the seat on the wine-colored sofa gratefully.

"No. But I'm trying to lose a few extra pounds and cake won't help."

"Why?" He was staring at her, she realized. A curious all-knowing stare that saw right to the heart of her.

"Well, cake has a lot of extra calories and fat that..."

"I mean, why are you trying to lose weight? You're not fat." His eyes skimmed down her tall figure in the loose cotton sundress. "And I should know. I saw you in that bathing suit, remember?"

Sasha did remember and his words sent a bolt of awareness through her body that sizzled as she felt the air fill with tingling undercurrents.

"Well..." She blushed. "Thank you. But I am kind of large and—" She never got any further.

Jake Windsor leaned forward to stare directly into her green eyes. "No," he corrected softly. "You're tall. So am I. What's wrong with that?"

"N-nothing," she stammered, unable to break away from the compelling stare in those clear gray eyes. "It's just that I have to watch out for any extra pounds that try to slip onto my hips."

It was embarrassing and Sasha wished she had never begun the discussion.

"Baloney." She started at the sharply bitten word. "The pace you move would scare any fat away from even the idea of settling there." His eyes were moving over that area of her anatomy with careful scrutiny. "Anyway, I don't understand all this concern women have over body size. If you're healthy, who cares?"

She watched the wide shoulders shrug and thought how wonderful his wife must have found it to be married to a man who gave so little thought to her dimensions. Dwain, on the other hand, had continually warned her about eating any and everything, but most especially chocolate. As if she would ever willingly give up chocolate! Sasha tossed the thought away. She was finished with Dwain.

"Here." Jake thrust out one of the four dark chocolate cupcakes he balanced on a huge white napkin. "Eat it."

So she did.

"Did you call Mrs. Natini to play the organ?" she asked after a few moments, anxious to restore the conversation to more normal footing.

"Done." He licked his fingers clean of the sticky sweet icing.

"And the ladies know about the lunch?"

He frowned at her. "I am organized in my work, you know," he chided. "It's all taken care of."

She quirked one eyebrow.

"Don't start spieling off that vainglorious speech to me," she chided archly. "I think people who boast are hiding some huge insecurities." She hid her smile at his affronted look.

"Anyway, aren't you afraid that somehow, in all the festivities, some unscrupulous person will snatch you up to the altar and have you say the words 'I do'?" She grinned at him teasingly, enjoying the startled look on his rugged face.

But Jacob Windsor didn't find her humor funny in the least. "I'll never remarry," he told her solemnly. "It's totally impossible." His face had that stern uncompromising look again. He motioned to the soda. "If you're finished?"

The hint was about as subtle as you could get and Sasha swallowed the urge to laugh. Prickly and proud, Jake Windsor was telling her to get out. It was sort of funny!

"Yes, I do have to get back to work," she said, stretching up from her chair. "I want to make a really nice setting in the hall." She frowned. "Why do they need the hall if it's a spur-of-the-moment deal and they're not local?"

He ambled along beside her, holding the door open for her to pass through.

"I gather they were here for the weekend and decided to just go ahead and do it. They spent an hour telephoning and then asked if I knew who could prepare a cold meal for fifty people."

He shrugged, the denim fabric pulling tight across his shoulders. As she watched him heft up the heaviest boxes, Sasha quenched the flash of awareness that raced through her when his arms flexed to take the weight.

"I gather the ladies said yes?"

He nodded, stuffing everything into the back of her car. "Yes. Mrs. Garner said cold cuts and salads would be very simple for them to handle. She even took Cody along to butter buns. I just hope that bratty kid isn't there with him. He's trouble."

Sasha choked back a laugh.

"It's Bratley," she told him. "Bobby Bratley." She grinned up at him, enjoying the joke. "But he certainly fits your description. And he would definitely put the kibosh on any festivities."

Jake smiled at her colorful word.

"These little peccadilloes of yours are interesting," he murmured. "You use words like other people use tools."

"'Peccadilloes'? The derivative of that term is Latin in origin," she told him, frowning severely. "From the verb 'to sin.' I don't think I like what you're inferring."

Jake burst out laughing then, a hearty, boisterous laugh that did wonders to the hard lines of his face.

"I didn't mean to call you a sinner." He chuckled, lifting his eyebrows. "But after all, if the shoe fits..."

"Well, I never!" She faked outrage. Seconds later she joined in the laughter, enjoying the easy repartee. It was refreshing to share a joke with someone who didn't mete out mirth in tiny portions of barely concealed disgust. For some reason a picture of Dwain's dull—no, nonexistent—

sense of humor flashed through her mind and she grinned with relief.

Her shoulder brushed against Jake's chest as she turned to slam the trunk closed. She felt the soft, delicate graze of the hairs on his arm tingle across her skin, and watched as his eyes narrowed in awareness.

And the laughter died.

He stood there staring at her as if there was something caught in her hair, his mouth mere inches from her own, his chocolaty breath mixing with hers. Sasha brushed her hand awkwardly over the short shiny spikes but when she felt nothing her hand dropped to her side.

She couldn't seem to free her gaze from the study of his intently serious gray eyes as they held hers. A current of hot, zinging electricity traveled from him to her that caused a strangely weak reaction in her knees and her breath to come in short, shallow gasps.

Sasha Lambert had never been as totally aware of any man as she was of Jake Windsor. Although she tried to regain that elusive sense of control that had always been her trademark, it wasn't easy to pretend nonchalance. When he leaned toward her, she held her breath, forcing her traitorous body to stand still. Then his mouth was on hers, the soft skin of his lips grazing her yearning ones, fulfilling all her fantasies. Microseconds later he jerked away, leaving her standing there, embarrassed.

"I, uh, I have to get moving," she stammered, easing past him to tug open the door as disappointment washed through her. "Are you coming?"

Jake moved, finally. But just to one side.

"Yes," he answered softly, eyes averted. "Since I dumped this mess on you, the least I could do is give you a hand. But I'll walk. I need the exercise." The last was added on as an afterthought, one long, slim finger tracing his bottom lip.

Sasha couldn't think of anything to say. Nothing seemed

appropriate and, anyway, her heart wouldn't stop that silly thudding. So she merely nodded and drove slowly across town, ordering her tingling senses to calm down as she rolled past the playground full of boisterous children enjoying their freedom.

So he was good-looking? So what? It didn't mean anything. Just because her heart was thudding away like a jackhammer was no reason to think he reciprocated her interest. Anyway, Jake Windsor had made it more than clear that he had no intention of getting involved. With anyone.

So why is he giving off these mixed signals?

It was a good question. Unfortunately she didn't have an answer. And no time to ponder the question further. There was only a little over an hour until the wedding began.

Sasha carried in the boxes of streamers and unfurled the royal blue and cream bells as she considered the best arrangement. While she organized her decorations, she heard Cody talking to someone in the kitchen.

"My dad says God always answers our prayers," he was asserting loudly.

"He didn't answer no prayer of mine," Bobby Bratley answered scornfully.

"Whatcha been prayin' for?" Cody demanded.

"For church to be canceled so I could go fishin'!"

Sasha grinned at the child's vehement reply.

"I already been fishing," Cody boasted smugly. "An' Sasha cooked them for us. It was great."

There was the clanging sound of a metal container hitting the floor.

"Oops! Sorry, Mrs. Garner. I sure am glad that the pot was empty." Bobby sounded properly repentant but one never knew with that boy.

"I been prayin' for a birthday party." Cody's voice was soft and Sasha wouldn't have heard it had she not been arranging the streamers near the kitchen door.

"Ya don't gotta pray for that," Bobby scolded him. "Ya

just gotta ask yer mom. Or yer dad.'' He'd added the last part as an afterthought, she noticed ruefully.

"Uh-uh." Cody sounded dismally sad. "My dad wouldn't like me to ask. Maybe if I had a mom, it'd be different. She'd know what to do, like my grandma did. We had lotsa kids over when we lived with her." There was a hint of nostalgia in his childish tones that tugged at her heartstrings. "My dad doesn't like kids much. 'Cept me."

There was a long silence then and Sasha crept away from the door, ashamed to be caught listening in. Jake came bounding through the back door shortly after, windblown and out of breath.

"What should I do?" he asked, eyeing the ladder she had leaned against the wall unsteadily, avoiding her gaze completely. It was obvious that he was also ignoring the current of tingling awareness that ran between them and she had no intention of reminding him.

Sasha showed him where to attach the streamers and soon they had the ceiling covered with ivory and blue streamers and iridescent blue helium balloons that she had filled from the portable tank in her car. The tables were already set up, which made it easier for them to secure everything to a huge heart-shaped centerpiece that hung down over the head table.

"Now I just have to embellish this table and everything is ready from my end," she told him, pleased at the lovely party look they had created. "Oh, my gosh, it's almost five. You'd better go and get changed. Here—" she tossed him her keys "—take my car. You haven't got much time to spare."

Jake mumbled and bumbled about being beholden or some such nonsense but in the end Sasha won.

"It's quarter to," she told him pertly, hands on her hips. "You'd better boogie. You can drop the car off later."

He boogied.

Sasha hummed the "Wedding March" as she draped the silk ivy along the length of the head table and then wove in an assortment of flowers. There were crystal goblets for the bride and groom and plain plastic ones for the rest. Tall tapers sat at the ready with blue foil matches nearby.

On each of the other tables she placed a rose bowl with several wild roses floating inside on a bit of tulle and an array of candles. It didn't matter that the candles were all different sizes and shapes, she decided as her eyes studied the effect. Each one added an air of festivity to the room and they would look lovely glowing in the dimly lit hall.

In front of every place setting she laid one of the tiny ivory scrolls that were held rolled up by a simple gold band. Inside was a lovely poem about the marriage customs of other lands that Sasha carried in Bednobs as staple wedding stock.

One more check to be sure the cake was positioned exactly in the center of the head table and then she stood back to admire her work.

"My, my, Sasha. You have such a talent for weddings." Vera Bratley eased her way through the entrance with a huge tray of cold cuts. "Everything looks lovely, dear."

Suddenly there was a terrific crash from the kitchen and they both hurried across the tile floor to find the source.

"Oh, no!"

Pastel-colored dessert squares of every description lay scattered across the counters and floors of the room. Three women and two small boys stared at the damage.

"I told you two to leave that food alone," Mrs. Garner scolded angrily, flushed and disheveled in the busy kitchen. "Now we're going to have to search for extras."

She was frowning fiercely at the two five-year-olds who were backing up as she advanced.

"Disobedience, that's all it is. Sheer disobedience."

"I didn't do it," Bobby bellowed, pushing Cody's

skinny form forward. "Cody was reaching to get one and he tipped..."

"Oh, Bobby!" Mrs. Bratley grabbed her son's arm and tugged him toward her. Unfortunately, his outflung arm caught a jar of pickles and knocked them to the floor. Glass and pickle juice spread everywhere.

Very Bratley looked about to cave in, Sasha decided. It was time to take matters into her own hands. Otherwise the wedding guests would starve. Or worse—they'd eat dill pickles on top of mushy nanaimo bars!

"Okay, guys. Here's the deal. You stand perfectly still until we get this mess cleaned up. Got it?" Sasha fixed them with her stern look and they nodded, suddenly silent. "Vera, you sweep up the glass and Esther can mop. I'll pick up the squares."

They worked together to clean up what was left of the lunch.

"We'll have to stop till the floor dries," Esther complained, staring at the empty dessert tray. "I just can't imagine what we'll do now. I cleaned everyone out of baked goods this morning and it's too late to go to the city."

The two ladies stared at Sasha disconsolately as she busied herself with the two troublemakers while a half-formed idea bubbled in her brain.

"I think you two owe Mrs. Garner an apology," she chided softly. "She was trying to help out and you caused an awful lot of extra work."

"I'm sorry, Mrs. Garner. I didn't mean to ruin your supper." Cody was tearfully apologetic and received a big hug from his caregiver.

Bobby was another story.

"I don't gotta apola...say I'm sorry when I didn't do nothin'," he blustered.

"That's lying," Cody complained loudly. "You climbed up—"

Sasha burst into the conversation quietly. "Well, that sure is too bad, Bobby, because I had something special planned. If you're not going to apologize, well then...I guess the fishing's off for today."

She turned as if to leave and smiled when she heard the gruff little voice mutter, "I guess I'm sorry, too, Mrs. Garner."

"Good," Sasha murmured. "Now I'm only going to say this once and if you don't obey, you will not go anywhere but home to bed. Got it?"

They nodded solemnly.

"Good. Go outside and sit down on the grass. I'll be there in a few minutes. If you're not sitting down when I get there, I'll forget about the picnic, too."

They dashed through the door in a rush, sending the punch bowl teetering. Fortunately Mrs. Bratley, well used to her son's rapid pace, steadied the pink confection easily.

"Now, ladies." Sasha eyed what was left of the dainties. "Here's what we're going to do."

She outlined the plan carefully for them and grinned as the relief crossed their faces.

"Sherbet," Mrs. Garner crowed. "I don't know why we didn't think of it. And with one of those little chocolate triangles stuck on top it'll look real elegant."

With quick, sure fingers they slipped the remaining dainties onto a big silver tray and tucked it away on one of the shelves.

"If someone wants lunch later," Mrs. Garner murmured, "we'll serve those. Otherwise, let's just freeze them for the next time this happens." She grinned at Vera Bratley. "And you know it will happen again," she chuckled.

Relieved that peace was restored once more, Sasha moved to the back door. And she almost got through it.

"Just a darn minute, Miss Sasha Lambert." Agatha McMurtry sounded hot and Sasha knew with a sinking heart exactly why. "Just what, exactly, is my daughter's wedding cake doing set up on that head table?'' the elderly woman demanded. "I paid good money for that cake and…"

The soft, pudgy hands were fluttering wildly and from her red face, it was evident that the woman's blood pressure had soared. Sasha slipped a chair behind her and urged her to sit.

"I can explain everything, Mrs. McMurtry. You just relax for a minute."

Think fast, she told herself. And you had better make it good. It occurred to her that Jake would love to hear the confession that went along with this big lie.

"I had a rush order for this wedding and I was working on that when I had a whole new idea for Darla's wedding. One that is much less expensive but really very elegant."

She crossed her fingers behind her back as the lie eased past her lips. "I tried to get hold of Darla but there just wasn't time. These people offered to pay top dollar and since I didn't want to see you stuck, I decided to use what I could for this wedding." She patted the older woman's shoulder.

"You can consider Darla's decorations paid in full if she accepts my ideas," she whispered softly. "It will be much more economical to do it this way and I think she'll really like the idea."

Nail the last one in your coffin, Sasha's subconscious laughingly mocked her. "I saw the idea in the latest issue of *Bride's* magazine."

As she had known it would, that seemed to cinch the matter and Agatha McMurtry stood to her swollen feet with a relieved smile.

"You just go ahead, dear," she murmured with a relieved sigh. "I know you'll do a lovely job."

Once she actually made it outside the door, Sasha heaved a sigh of heartfelt relief. At last! Now maybe she could relax. She sprawled on the grass and closed her eyes, enjoying the whir of insects hovering nearby on the hot prairie breeze. Everything smelled fresh and clean and full of spring promise, she mused as the bright green maples fluttered overhead.

Spring—a time of promise, of planning for the future. She wondered idly what her future held. Her fingers plucked a stem of grass as she pondered the years ahead.

Would it always be someone else's wedding she was worrying about? she asked the clear blue sky. Was she never to hear the frail cry of a newborn baby, or feel its warmth in her empty arms?

Get a grip, she warned herself. *Good things come to those who wait.* She snorted at the ridiculous phrase.

Good things happen to those who go out and get them, she retorted. *And I will have a child. I will.*

She was thinking about the pastor and how his dark good looks would mix with hers when she heard the sound. A kind of smothered sigh. The boys!

Sasha jumped to her feet, suddenly aware of how much time had passed since the children had been sent outside. Her heart dropped back into place when she saw them sitting on the grass watching her.

"Is it time to go now?" Cody asked softly.

"Yeah! We been sittin' here for hours," Bobby wailed.

Sasha cast them a stern look. "For your little performance in there you should be grounded. For the summer. Snitching brownies, indeed!"

Their faces fell and she eyed them severely. "How many did you take?"

Cody held up six fingers. Bobby two.

Sasha stared down the terror of Allen's Springs. "How many Bobby?"

Finally he grinned shamefacedly.

"Ten."

"I hope you get sick," she told them both smugly. Fortunately, the two had never looked healthier.

"I really am sorry," Cody muttered. "I can go back and 'polagize." He started toward the back door.

"No!" Sasha grabbed his arm just before he got the door open. "I think they know you're sorry," she quipped, guiding him away from a second bout of dessert warfare.

Heaven only knew what Esther Garner would do if yet another child-engineered tragedy befell the First Avenue Church ladies' group. Their reputation was at stake with this wedding.

Sasha relented her stern stance. "Come on, guys. Let's go fishing."

As they whooped and hollered down the street toward her house, Sasha mentally chided her tired muscles.

This is what it's like to have kids, remember, she told herself. Get used to it.

Chapter Five

"Stop tossing up all the stupid, unimportant impediments you can conceive of and listen to what I'm saying. Cody wants a birthday party." Sasha glared daggers at Pastor Jake's reclining figure, but the reverend appeared to be less than thrilled with her idea.

"It's very nice of you to think of Cody," he murmured from under the straw hat covering his face. She watched his long, lean body wiggle in the chaise longue just a bit before his next words slammed her against his cool resistance. "Someday, when you have children, Miss Lambert, you will learn that you cannot possibly give them everything they ask for."

Sasha was aghast and not a little frustrated that he was trying to make this personal. She was also fed up with always being on the outside looking in. Just for once it would have been so nice to be too involved with her own family to help out Reverend Windsor's orphaned son.

"But he only wants a birthday party. What's so hard about that?"

Jake tipped the hat away from his eyes to glare at her.

"I've asked Mrs. Garner to make something special for dinner tomorrow night, I bought him several new outfits, and we're going to go for a drive later. Satisfied?" The gray eyes glared up at her.

Sasha was appalled. "No!" Her voice was loud and she dropped it down just a bit at the turbulent look that was washing over his hard face.

"A *special* supper, a new shirt and a drive," she snorted. "It sounds like the kid is going on sixty instead of six." The only response she received was a settling of the hat over his face and the sound of soft but very unsubtle snoring.

It made her mad. Flaming hot and insensibly mad. Without thinking, she bent and quickly tipped the chaise longue, depositing the good reverend and his straw hat on the grass with a thud.

"Hey!" Jake rose to his full height with the fury of a man whose peaceful Sunday afternoon in the sun has just been disrupted. He was not a happy camper, Sasha observed smugly.

"You're a juggernaut," he muttered, straightening the chair and replacing its cushion. "Barreling along, crushing everything in your path, forcing us all to do your will."

Sasha made a face at him. "Thank you, oh, great one," she mocked sweetly. "I do know the meaning of the word."

"Oh, good." He grinned smugly.

Sasha frowned. Up until she'd met Jake Windsor, she had always liked word games. But lately he'd been one-upping her just a little too often.

How could she have ever thought she wanted to kiss the man? What she really wanted, Sasha muttered to herself, was to smack his self-satisfied face. Instead she curled her fingers into tight fists by her sides. Arrogant male!

"Sticks and stones," she muttered, red-faced. It was childish but she couldn't think of anything else more appropriate at the moment. To her disgust he burst out laughing.

"Really, Sasha. Such language. And totally otiose, er, unnecessary in this case," he murmured kindly at the confused look on her face.

"Look, can we just stick to plain old English," she said coldly. "I came here to ask you what you were going to do for Cody's birthday. I happened to overhear him talking and he said that he's been praying for a birthday party. I just wondered if you were going to grant his wish."

"I can't answer all his prayers. After all, I am not God, Sasha." Jake glared at her from his seat on the longue.

"*I* certainly never suggested that there was any such resemblance," she snickered.

He winced at the shot. A great whoosh of air puffed out the breadth of his chest admirably.

"What are you suggesting for my son's birthday, Miss Lambert?" It was not a nice tone of voice for a pastor to use and Sasha decided to call him on it later. For now, though, there was Cody's party to contemplate.

"I merely thought it would be nice to have a little party. You know, kids, birthday cake, games, presents. Invite a few of the kids from Allen's Springs, maybe six or so."

He shook his head slowly as if to clear it. Sasha felt the stab of awareness all the way to her toes when his arm brushed hers as he waved it around. Her knees were weak and so she sank onto the grass. It was ridiculous. The most innocent touch had her quivering with excitement. Anyone would think she was desperate for a man's touch, she scorned her feverish pulse.

Not any man, her subconscious chided. *Just this one.*

Stop it, she commanded. Concentrate on the issue at hand. Jake was speaking.

"Do you really think I *need* to have six screaming children running around my yard, spilling food all over and wreaking havoc wherever they go just to realize my son is getting older? And do you honestly think I'm the type of person who actually *knows* any children's games?'

Sasha studied him seriously. Her tone was soft but firm.

"I think you'd better learn some quickly," she told him soberly. "Before Cody is too old to have a birthday party with kids running all over. Before he's all grown up and gone."

Jake studied her face as if he were seriously contemplating the future and didn't like what he saw in it.

"I think you need to give him very good memories that will carry him through some rough times ahead. And I'm not sure a special supper and a drive will do it." Sasha leaned forward in her intensity, her green eyes glowing as she spoke.

"Cody wants to be like the other kids around here. Okay, he doesn't have a mother and you're not about to get him a replacement anytime soon. Fine. That's up to you. But couldn't you at least make some parts of his life normal?" Sasha tried to explain her empathy for the child's lonely existence that had driven her to seek Jake's reluctant figure out on a solitary Sunday afternoon. "He wants to be like Bobby—"

"God forbid!" He interrupted her, a look of terror crossing his stern features.

Sasha ignored him and continued. "With a family that argues sometimes, sure. But deep down each one knows they still care for the other and that they'll try, come hell or high water, to take care of their own."

"Are you suggesting that I rent some children to live here?" He derided her with disgust.

He watched her rise to her full height, anger tinting her cheekbones a dull red. She was no retiring wimp, that was for sure! Jake decided he liked a woman who stood up for herself.

"I'm suggesting that you start thinking of your child and his needs instead of your poor little widowed self," she flung angrily, obviously fed up with his mocking tones. "I can't imagine why you think any self-respecting female would be after such an egocentric, egotistical, stingy man like you."

She strode across the lawn to the high wooden gate and yanked it open. "You can't even forget your own comfort long enough to think about a little boy who only wants to have a special cake and some friends on his birthday."

Sasha glared at him furiously. "You don't deserve to have a son," she exhorted and then slammed the gate shut behind her departing figure. "Men!"

Jake jumped up from his seat, seething at her scathing tone. How dare she criticize him? She had no idea of the things he had done to make Cody's life better.

Without a second thought he raced across the lawn and through the gate, grabbing her arm before she could turn the corner of his house.

It was ridiculous. One touch and his body was zinging with electricity. Jake gave in to the whirlwind of emotions coursing through him and kissed her. Hard. On the mouth, with every bit of frustration and emotion that was roiling around inside of him. Seconds later he reproached himself for his stupidity.

"Just a darn minute here," he stormed, puffing at the exertion and the wrath and a lot of unexplained feelings. He hung on to her arm, yanking her slim form forward and swallowing suddenly as she pressed against him for a moment. "A birthday isn't the only thing Cody wants. He also wants a mother. So there! Am I supposed to get that for him, too?"

He groaned inwardly. Now why did you have to let that out? He castigated himself.

Sasha's green eyes slashed down to where his fingers bit into the white skin of her forearm. Her black eyebrows tilted up at him.

"*If* you don't mind," she said frostily.

"I certainly do mind," he rasped, tugging her back into the yard and beyond his neighbors' curious eyes.

He slammed the gate shut with a ringing finality and stood in front of it lest the hot-tempered vixen facing him attempt another getaway. And he wasn't apologizing for kissing her, he told himself angrily. No way!

"In the first place, since you're so set on learning new words, technically I'm a widower, not a widow."

She rolled her eyes, her wide mouth pursed into a thin line. Jake studied her face and wondered why he hadn't noticed before just how gorgeous Sasha Lambert was when she got mad.

Her black hair glistened in the sun, shooting off sparks that glinted in her eyes. Thick, black, sooty lashes were perfect frames for those wide, jagged jade eyes. She directed the piercing glare to stab at him and he swore he could feel them slash across his skin when she fixed her sights on his face.

Loosening his hold fractionally, he tugged her to one of the cedar chairs at the round picnic table and gently pushed her toward it, pulling his hands away when they would have smoothed down her arms.

"Sit down," he ordered, and then amended as that mutinous look returned to her face, "Please?"

He smiled to himself when she eased her long slim body onto the chair and sat rigidly perched on the edge of it, ready for flight. So far and no further, he mused silently. Fine. He sat on the seat facing her and sucked in a deep breath. Where to begin?

"Look, Sasha," he breathed. "I'm not quite the troglodyte you think I am." Sasha's eyebrows raised at the word, but other than that, Jake could see no response to his effort to explain. He tried again.

"I'm not totally stuck in the past. Neither am I grieving for something I can't have. I know Cody wants a party. He recites it every night. It's not exactly easy to miss." He shrugged. "He also wants that water pistol thing that has a tank that straps on the back. You can drown your opponent at fifty feet." Jake grinned dryly. "The toy is no problem. I can buy that."

He stared at his hands, trying to force the words out. But there was no easy way to say this without admitting that he needed a woman's help and that was exactly what he was loathe to ask for.

Bite the bullet, his mind ordered. *Just get it over with.*

"But I never gave a child a birthday party. I don't know what to do and I'd probably screw it all up. I'm just not very good with kids, I guess."

"Bull!"

He was shocked. "I beg your pardon?"

"You should," she said smartly. "For a whole lot of things. But right now we're talking about Cody."

He watched as she sank back into her chair, as if deep in thought, and crossed her long slim legs, tugging her yellow shorts down to properly cover her smooth golden thighs. Jake knew he was ogling her as he admired the curve of those legs. She had a racer's body, he thought. Tall and lean and quick. And very feminine with the curves in all the right places, as he'd felt for himself a few moments ago.

He jerked his attention back to what she was saying, deriding himself for his less than professional interest in the gorgeous woman sitting in his yard.

"Kids are just like new little plants," she told him. "They want someone to talk to, to feel safe with, to explore with. They want to feel special and nurtured. And they want to feel like they're the best thing since sliced bread."

He stared at the impassioned look on her beautiful face, at the glow on her fair skin.

"How do you come to all this knowledge, may I ask? You don't have any children." He watched curiously as her face lit up with a huge grin.

"For as long as I can remember there were tons of kids hanging around—our home, the street, whatever." She told him this as her eyes stared off into the distance. "Our family was large and there was always someone staying over. At one point in my life I just wanted to get away and be on my own." He started at her harsh laugh. "That lasted about six months. Until I got to college and realized how boringly organized it was. I missed my family, the mayhem."

As he watched, Sasha tugged at the shorts once more but without much success. They stayed where they were, comfortably hugging her thighs and Jake couldn't seem to move his eyes away. He listened as she continued.

"I started baby-sitting for a little spare money and soon found that the professors' wives would pay a hefty salary for a nanny in the summer months." She grinned up at him. "I loved it. I could sit around the pool, go to the beach or travel and all I had to do was play games with one or two little kids."

He shuddered. "It sounds terribly exhausting." Anyone who looked less exhausted than the vibrantly alive woman beside him couldn't be imagined. "What did you do once you got out on your own and went to work?"

She shrugged, her slim shoulders moving slightly.

"Oh, I got caught up in the usual scene, but after a while, I began to realize how fake it all seemed." She frowned, her beautiful face drawn in perplexity. "Everyone pretended to be having a wonderful time, but they weren't any happier than I was after the late parties and the bar hopping. And they were still alone. Eventually I got my priorities straight and moved out here."

"And now?" He watched her closely, searching for the answers that hung in the back of his mind to questions he wouldn't admit to having.

"Now, I want my own children to raise. I want to do all the things with them that my mother never had time to do with me. Children are wonderful teachers and they're so full of life and love. They only want you to focus totally and exclusively on them. Not too hard, is it?''

He snorted. ''Are you kidding?''

She nodded slowly, her head tipped back as she let the sun cascade over her face. ''Okay, so it's tough. And your problem is?''

Jake felt as if he were a bratty little boy who was being reprimanded for something. Thing was, he did feel guilty. And inadequate. She was speaking again.

''Get beyond all that. Think of Cody and how proud he would be to have his dad hold a birthday party for him. He doesn't care that you don't know any games. He just wants his friends to come to his house like he goes to theirs.''

Jake closed his eyes, trying to dislodge the picture of total chaos that he knew would ensue.

''Okay, Rev,'' she challenged. ''What's the worst that could happen at this party, if you decide to have one?''

Now her eyes had darkened to a deep forest green and they were boring into him, maligning his fear. Jake didn't like that look one little bit. His pride forced him to defend himself.

''They could destroy my home,'' he muttered, glaring back at her.

''Six little boys?'' Sasha hooted with glee. ''You have the nerve to think you can keep your thumb on the whole congregation when you can't manage a party for a few *children?*''

He hated that scathing tone of voice, Jake decided. It wasn't in the least attractive. And he hated it even more that she had tapped, albeit unknowingly, into his biggest fear. He forced a smile to his lips.

''Sasha, this isn't even my house. We are only using what has been provided by the church.''

She snapped her fingers in his face. ''So you rebuild. So what? Next problem.''

The pressure was building now and Jake clenched his fists in frustration. His jaw hurt, it was so tightly gritted. He eased up a bit and unclenched his back teeth. In the process, that light, haunting fragrance she wore wove around him, adding to his frustration.

"Miss Lambert. You are now talking about inviting into my home a boy who put hair remover into his sister's hair gel container. The same boy who sprinkled itching powder on the toilet paper at church and who dribbled Krazy Glue on the chairman of the board's seat before the last meeting."

He raked a hand through his hair as he glared at her.

"Do you really think I want to invite this…this…fiend into *my* home for an entire afternoon?"

A beautiful smile curved her lips. Jake shook his head tiredly. What was so danged funny? He tried again.

"I might add that Bobby purchased both the itching powder and the glue from you." He frowned at her. "I'm not sure you're qualified to give anyone advice about children."

He had to give her credit. She didn't take the least bit of offense.

"Just goes to show what an imaginative mind the child has," she told him cheerfully. "Actually, Bobby is very bright. He just needs some planned activities to occupy his time. And he's Cody's friend."

She said it as if that settled the matter and for the hundredth time Jake wondered why God had ever chosen him for the town of Allen's Springs. Someone should have warned him about Sasha Lambert, he decided grimly. It was a duty the chamber of commerce couldn't ignore.

Jake shook his head, shrugging his shoulders in defeat. "I give in," he muttered sadly, feeling as if she had bested him yet again. "What do you want me to do?" He scowled across the table at her, surprised when she vehemently shook her head.

"Oh, no, you don't," she told him. "This is supposed to be a party *you* give for *your* son. The most I can help with is the cake."

"What!" Jake surged to his feet. "You…you con artist. You drop me into this and then you just walk away?" He glared at her. "No way, lady." He poured them each a glass of the chilled iced tea Mrs. Garner had left.

"Sit there and drink that," he ordered. "I'm going to get a pen and paper. Make no mistake about it, Miss Lambert. You are going to help with this birthday party."

She helped, all right. Boy did she help! By the time Sasha left two hours later, Jake wondered why he'd ever allowed himself to even consider the idea of a birthday party. Hot dogs over a fire he could handle. Even making lemonade wasn't a problem. Sasha would get the cake and he and Bobby could go to her store and pick out the decorations and stuff for something she called "goodie bags."

That wasn't what worried him. The biggest problem, as far as Jake could tell, was what six wild, hoydenish children would do for two hours? Sasha, with her advice, hadn't been much help, either.

"What kind of things did you do at Cody's other parties?"

She'd asked the question so innocently, yet Jake had felt a shaft of pain reach deep into his soul. He hadn't been present for Cody's second birthday. Angela and Cody had celebrated on their own. And the third had slid past without any fuss whatsoever, following so closely on the heels of Angela's death. Then his mother had handled everything for the past two years and he'd had little input into the event. Jake suddenly realized how much time he'd missed spending with his own son.

"The best parties, at least the ones I've helped with, are the ones that take place away from the child's home," she'd told him, peering off into space. "You can put the gifts in the car so that nothing gets lost or broken.'' She'd met his gaze seriously while relaying the information.

"Then your child can play with them when he has more time to appreciate each one. Also, the other children don't seem to be quite so destructive if they're involved in something out of doors.''

He'd frozen on the word ''destructive'' and consequently heard little else the woman had to say. Remnants of the shock he'd felt when she stood to go, leaving him sitting there with a mile-long list, left an addled feeling squeezing his brain that only barely abated as she'd gently patted his tense shoulder. His mixed-up brain did telegraph that he enjoyed her gentle touch. Surprise, surprise!

"You'll do fine,'' she'd told him softly. ''Just remember that you're doing this for Cody and that'll make all the difference.''

She'd turned to go then, golden legs glinting in the sun. He'd been so entranced by her shining eyes and slim elegant body Jake had almost missed her last words.

"If you get really stuck,'' she'd said softly, ''I'll be a phone call away.'' She had sauntered across the lawn with the long-legged grace he noticed every time she moved. Turning at the gate, Sasha had spoken confidently. ''But I really think that if you get Cody in on the planning and remember that it's his party, you'll be a big hit.''

Jake thought he'd nodded; he may have even said thank-you. But he was alone when the terror gripped his whirling brain and paralyzed him in his chair.

Six children, and all of them shades of Bobby Bratley! His fingers gripped the condensating glass like an anchor as he closed his eyes.

"Oh, God... Heeeelp!''

"Dad?''

Jake opened his eyes to find his son staring at him.

"Are you okay, Daddy?'' Cody's chubby hand patted him on the leg gently. ''Are you sick?''

He had the anxious look of a child who knows he has only one parent left to look after him. It was that look of fear that shook Jake to his very core.

She was right, he decided brusquely. Sasha Lambert had been right on the money when she had called him self-centered. He was the parent here. He was supposed to look after the child; not vice versa.

He surged to his feet in a burst of newfound strength. Well, then, he'd do it. He'd show her and himself that he was a darned good parent. Totally dedicated to the well-being of his son.

And if that resulted in damage to life, limb and the manse, so be it!

Sasha groaned awake at the sound of Oreo's sharp woof. The dog never barked. Never. Something must be the matter.

Her eyes peered through the darkness to the gleaming red numbers on her bedside clock. It was 1:25—*a.m.* She tugged the sheet away tiredly and climbed out of bed, slipping her feet into the floppy sandals by the bed. There was no need to turn on the light. She knew the placing of every piece of furniture by heart.

As she moved silently through the house, she felt the cool whisper of the evening breeze caress her face.

Good! The rooms were cooling off at last. It had been a scorcher today and even the most dedicated users of Allen's Springs mineral spa had left the warm salty water to browse through her shop. Of course Saturdays were always busy, but today she'd been glad of Deidre and the two teenage girls she had recently hired to man the store while she taught a class of kids how to make sand art pictures.

Outside, the lawn was cool and damp, brushing her ankles with its wetness. She strode over to the dog's run, speaking as she moved.

"What is it, girl? Did somebody bother you?"

Sasha peered into the darkness beyond her fence, but only the empty stretch of town park yawned blackly beyond. Which was a good thing, Sasha decided, remembering the short cotton gown she wore. It had been so hot and she'd been so tired, it had felt good to slip on the cool, thigh-length wisp of white cotton. Sleeveless with a dipping V neck, it allowed her skin to breathe freely.

But it wasn't meant to be worn out of doors and she hadn't thought to grab a robe. She cast a quick look around to be sure no one was watching from nearby.

"Like who would be out watching for women in their nightgowns at this time of night," she scolded herself.

The dog barked once in response and scraped at something in front of her. Sasha bent to get a better look and then squealed loudly as the thing jumped at her.

"Yikes! What in the world…" She scrambled backward to regain her footing. The dog was barking furiously now and pawing at the ground. "Quiet, Oreo. Now let's see…why it's a huge frog."

Evidently Oreo didn't care what the object was. All she seemed interested in was evicting the intruder from her pen. Sasha laughed.

"Okay, Oreo," she teased. "I'll fight the big ferocious frog for you." She scooped the amphibian up with one hand and carried it out the back gate. It hopped off, croaking dire predictions as it jumped across the back alley to find a new home. Oreo gave one last snort of disgust before returning to her house. She turned around three times and then curled into a ball, ready for sleep.

"Good night, girl." Sasha laughed, closing the gate of her pen. "Try and get some rest now."

A low growl rumbled in the dog's chest as she moved back toward the side of her pen. Sasha felt the hair on her arms stand on end. Someone was here!

"Who is it?" she called loudly, quaking in her slippers.

"It's me." The voice was low and slurred, but familiar.

"Dwain?" Sasha stared down in shock at the man flopped across her favorite chaise longue. "What are you doing here?"

His hand snaked out to wrap around her wrist, yanking her on top of him. "Come to see my best girl. Love of my life. Kiss me, baby."

Sasha tried to push away, but his hands were like bands of steel.

"Let me go, Dwain," she ordered, shoving hard against his chest. "You know very well that *you're* the love of your own life. And you've been drinking again!" This predisposition to use alcohol as a solution to his problems had been one reason she'd first started to question her choice of Dwain as husband material, she remembered.

He must have had quite a bit, Sasha decided, shifting her head away from the overpowering aroma of whiskey. His eyes had started to close and his fingers were loosening. With one last mighty push, she scrambled free.

"Wassah mattah?" he muttered, sitting up on the longue. "WhaddI do wrong?"

Sasha straightened her short gown and glared down at him. "You drank too much, that's all. Stay here, I'll go get you a cold glass of water."

Evidently he was too out of it to move because when she returned seconds later with the drink, Dwain lay snoring in her chair.

"Oh, no, you don't, bucko," she huffed, tugging his solid dead weight upright and locking the chair into position. "You're not spending the night here."

Sasha pressed the cup against Dwain's lips as she held his head. Some of the chilly liquid splashed onto his face and down his shirtfront.

"Wha..." His eyes opened to focus hazily on her gleaming white gown. "Want to see you," he murmured, tugging a handful of the cotton nearer.

"If you don't let go of me and get out of here fast, you'll be sorry," she muttered.

But Dwain had other ideas. He pulled her onto his lap and pressed his hot mouth against hers.

"Marry me, Sasha." His words were slurred, his hand pressing against the small of her back. "We could go traveling around the world together. You'd like to travel. And we wouldn't ever have to come back to Allen's Springs. Of course, we'd have to wait awhile."

Sasha resorted to using the full range of her height to push her would-be suitor roughly away. She splashed some more of the water over him. He was awake now, she noticed, and glaring at her balefully.

"Come on, Dwain. We've been all over this. You want a little woman who will be your hausfrau. You want someone you can show off and tell off, someone your mother will order around until her dying day."

Sasha wished desperately that she had a cup of strong black coffee just then. It looked like it would be a long night.

"I don't want to travel just to get away from someone. I could have done that when I lived in Toronto, but I left there because I wanted something different. I told you that if I got married, I'd want to settle down and have kids, a whole passel of them. You hate kids. Well, Dwain, I am going to have a child."

She glared down at him and noticed he was wide awake and gulping down the water. "But I'm also going to have my own life. You wouldn't like that. You'd want my life to revolve around yours." She shook her head. "I can't do that, Dwain. Even if I wanted to. I'm my own person. I can't be a doormat for any man. No matter who he is."

"I wouldn't boss you around." Dwain sounded petulant, like a spoiled little boy. Which he was. "And we wouldn't have to live with my mother forever, you know. I offered to get another house." He frowned at her. "Of course, it wouldn't have been as nice and we would have had to spend a lot on fixing it up. Seems a waste when mother's right there, waiting for us to move in with her.''

Sasha shuddered in the darkness, nauseated at the thought of living with Dwain's complaining, chronically unwell, perpetually nagging mother.

''No, Dwain. Thank you, but we've already agreed that it's better if we both go our separate ways. I can't be what you want in a wife and this isn't the time to discuss it. Go home and sober up.''

''There aren't a lot of men around here, you know,'' he said complacently.

''There aren't a lot of single women available, either, Dwain,'' she murmured. ''Especially not ones who would take on your mother.'' She hadn't meant for him to hear, but judging from the ugly look on his face, he had.

He muttered something uncomplimentary and Sasha heard alarm bells ringing in her brain.

''Pardon?'' At the unpleasant look on his face, Sasha wished she hadn't asked for a repeat of his remark.

''I said, you probably wouldn't be any good in bed anyway.'' He was standing now and reached one arm out to lock it around hers. He dragged her against him. ''Not like Maudie.''

She gasped at his temerity but that was all the time she had to think as his mouth moved nearer.

''Let's find out how knowledgeable you really are, Sasha, shall we?''

''No,'' she protested, ''we shan't.'' But his hands were strong. She turned her head away from his mouth and felt the wet slurpy kiss land on her neck.

''Come on, honey,'' he taunted. ''You want kids so bad, but I'll give you something you'll like better.''

She slapped his face then, hard and loud in the night air.

''Shame on you, Dwain. I never gave you cause to act

this way. I thought you had more respect for me than that."
She shoved hard and he stepped back unsteadily.

"You don't want me to father those children you're always yakking about but you go hanging around that minister as if you're in heat. Come on, just give me—"

Whatever else he'd been about to say was drowned in the spray of water from her garden hose. It had been a last resort and Sasha prayed that Dwain would come to his senses. He'd never been like this before and she was thankful their relationship had already ended.

"Go home and dry out, Dwain," she ordered firmly as he spluttered angrily in front of her. "And don't come here again. I have nothing more to say to you. Maybe you should look up Maudie again. She's more your type."

He surged toward her, an angry, hateful look in his eyes as he pushed past the stream of water she directed at him.

"I didn't come here to talk, anyway," he muttered as he turned off the faucet with a flick of his wrist. "And for sure not about Maudie. Every guy in town knows her preferences." He grinned nastily. "But nobody knows yours. Yet."

Fear, cold and clammy, crawled up her spine as Sasha realized she was alone, almost naked, with an angry drunk. What a fool she had been! This was a situation she had never dreamt of from Dwain.

"No, Dwain. Leave me alone. Go home to your mother."

He kept coming, determination engraved on his face.

"I think Sasha asked you to leave. Three times if I'm not mistaken."

They both whirled around at the soft, menacing tones. Sasha breathed a sigh of relief at the forbidding sight of the tall, muscular man looming at the edge of her yard.

"You'll be fortunate if Miss Lambert doesn't charge you with assault," Jake murmured softly. The steely edged tones were hard to ignore and it appeared that Dwain wouldn't try.

"Ah, all hail the conquering hero," he muttered angrily as his hands dropped away from Sasha's arms. "Come to take over from where I left off." Dwain sneered at the taller man with contempt. "Think you can do better than I can, do you?"

Jake didn't back off one inch. He merely fixed the man with that piercing gray stare.

"It wouldn't take much right now, would it?" Jake said archly, returning the insolent regard with a steady look. "You're drunk. You've just been exceedingly rude to someone who's never done you any harm, and now you're trying to force a woman into something she doesn't want." He smiled grimly. "No, I don't think it would take much to improve upon that."

Dwain studied the other man with a thoughtful frown before he turned back to face Sasha. His face was a sullen surly red.

"She and I have things to talk about. We're engaged."

"That's not what I heard." Jake offered the words quietly. "I understood the lady turned your offer down. You have no hold on her."

Sasha watched as Dwain stared at his feet, kicking the ground with one booted toe. As the cool night air swirled around them he seemed to sober up.

"I'm sorry. I should never have come here tonight. Shouldn't have been drinking, either. Can't hold it. I just figured maybe you could learn to love me if…" He stopped and began again. "Please forgive me, Sasha. I won't bother you anymore."

She nodded stiltedly, hands wrapped around her quivering body. She was cold, so cold.

"J-just go home now, okay? And don't drive."

He shook his head, a half smile tugging at the corners

of his mouth. "Always the little mama, eh, Sasha? Okay, I'll walk it off, I guess."

Jake watched the smaller man slink away and closed the gate carefully behind him. His eyes moved to Sasha, widening at the picture she made standing in the moonlight in the thin white transparent gown.

No wonder this Dwain fellow had gone off his rocker, he mused. She looked ethereal and unreal; sort of unworldly as she stood there staring blankly back at him. The gown had been liberally splattered with water and it clung, defining her shape through the thin fabric. He could see the swell of her full round breasts outlined clearly, nipples jutting out in the cool night air. The fabric dipped in at her waist and pasted wetly against her hips, caressing the slope of her buttocks like a lover.

Every nerve in Jake's hard body was on fire, pulsing with an aliveness that it hadn't known in three years. He was amazed to find himself aching to caress her, to pull her tall, shapely body into his arms and hold it close—protect her from the Dwains of the world and keep her to himself for his own private pleasure. It was a feeling he'd almost forgotten, buried beneath years of loss and denial.

But it had nothing to do with Angela. He knew that. She was dead and he was alive. Achingly so.

When his eyes moved to her face, Jake was jolted from his haze of desire by the vacant look in her beautiful green eyes. "Sasha?" He spoke softly and very gently. "Sasha, are you all right?"

Slowly her face turned upward to stare at him. She looked bemused, he decided, and then called himself an idiot as he remembered his first aid.

Shock, she was in shock. He knew that under other circumstances there was no way the fiery, determined woman he knew would stand there and be ogled by him or any other man without some type of gritty response.

"Sasha? Can you hear me?" At the touch of his hand

on her arm, she jumped back, away from him. Fear crowded into her face, which had drained of all color.

"It's okay. He's gone now. Dwain's gone." He repeated the words over and over, softly, soothingly, until her eyes focused on him.

"Gone? Are you s-sure?" Her hands were shaking now. In fact her entire body seemed to quiver in reaction.

"Yes, he's gone. Here, drink this." He pressed the glass of water she had placed on the patio table against her shaking hands and lifted them to her mouth. "It's okay now. Just sip it slowly. You're safe."

He tensed when his arm brushed against her breast as he helped her. Sasha seemed not to notice the touch, featherlight as it was, but Jake could feel the nerves burn the length of his arm. He ignored it. He had to.

You're her minister, he told himself. You are here to comfort and console her, not to add to her fear.

"Come and sit down," he murmured, and when she still stood standing where she was, he wrapped an arm around her waist and guided her to the longue.

She was shivering, Jake realized. He had no desire to upset her further so he pressed her body into the chair and rushed inside for a shawl or a blanket, anything to warm her up.

Everything was dark inside, not a light turned on, which probably meant the man had surprised her. He wondered why she would have ventured outside without a wrap and then decided to ignore the questions for now. He found her bedroom without meaning to, but that was okay since she had left a thick terry housecoat thrown across the end of the bed. Jake glanced only cursorily around the room but it was enough to tell him that this room was ultrafeminine with its white flounces and frills. Even the old fourposter had a white lacy canopy, he noted.

Sasha was still sitting on the side of the longue when he returned with the robe.

"Stand up for a minute, honey," he urged, and wrapped the fabric around her shaking body, trying to ignore his heightened awareness of her femininity.

Gently he drew the belt about her narrow waist and tied it carefully. Then all breathing stopped as she buried her head against his shoulder. Her arms twined themselves around his waist as she snuggled against his warmth.

"I was s-so s-scared," she whispered. "I thought h-he was going t-to…"

"I know," he murmured, smoothing his hand over her glossy head. To his surprise, Jake found her hair as silky soft as it looked. He soothed her with noncommittal noises as his hand brushed down her back, easing the racking sobs from her body.

"It's okay, honey. Cry it out." He whispered the endearments softly, fully conscious of the fact that he held a stunningly sexy woman in his arms and that the feel of those curves against him were igniting fires he had thought long since burnt out.

He had no intention of acting on his baser instincts, Jake told himself self-righteously. He only wanted to help her through this. And somehow, to do that he had to keep brushing his hand over her hair and down her back. He had to keep his arm wrapped around her narrow waist and support her weight against his. He grimaced. Some hardship!

The crying had given way to intermittent sobs that were even now dying out. Every so often she gave a little hiccup against him. When she made the slightest motion away, Jake forced his arms to let go and fall to his side.

"I'm sorry," she murmured, peeping up at him through those long black lashes. "I kind of fell apart there. I don't usually do that."

One finger reached out of its own volition and brushed the tears from her cheeks before Jake folded his length into the ratty old chair she had placed opposite the longue. He had to organize his thoughts before his mouth was capable of speaking.

"You had good reason," he said softly. "He was in a foul mood. I'm just glad I happened to be passing."

She looked up at that. "Just happened to be passing at one-thirty in the morning?" Her black brows frowned at him. "What about Cody?"

"It's past two now." Jake grinned, glancing at his watch. "Cody's on a sleep-over with Bobby," he told her smugly. "Anyway, Mrs. Garner would have been there. She sleeps in, remember?"

"Oh, yes. But what were you doing way over here?" Her voice might be shaky but she wasn't giving up easily. Jake felt his face flush and forced himself to marshal his embarrassed thoughts.

"Jogging in the park," he said at last. "I just got back from a bereavement call and I decided to go for a run to relax. I heard Oreo barking. By the time I got here, *he* was mauling you."

Sasha seemed to accept his words at face value and wiped her nose once more with the big handkerchief he'd provided.

"Well, thank you for helping me with him. I don't know whatever possessed him to act like that. In the six months we dated, he'd barely kissed me half a dozen times."

Jake decided he had no business feeling relieved at that. He hadn't heard much of their conversation, but he'd heard enough and he figured they had certainly done more than exchange a chaste kiss. Some of the sexual frustration he was feeling leeched out in his voice as he met her turbulent sea-foam gaze with his own.

"Maybe it was the outfit."

She flushed at that, hugging the robe a little closer.

"It is very, er, alluring," he mumbled, then wished he'd kept his mouth shut.

"It was never meant to be seen by a man," she retorted

hotly, her face showing a return of color in the wash of moonlight that streamed through the trees.

Jake wished he had never started the conversation. He felt rattled and ornery and even angry at the black-haired beauty in front of him in her virginal white robe.

"Not even by the man who seems only too willing to be the father of that child you want so desperately?" he demanded brusquely.

Chapter Six

Sasha gulped a mouthful of air and wondered if her brain was entirely clear yet. She looked up once more to find those gray eyes blazing down at her. "I'm sorry," she whispered breathlessly. "I don't think I heard you quite correctly. I must still be..."

"I asked if Dwain hadn't seen you in that fetching outfit before. Perhaps it led him to believe that you were offering more than friendship."

His face was a rigid mask of contempt, but in his eyes there was a spark of...jealousy? Impossible, she told herself. Why would Jake Windsor be jealous of Dwain?

"I have never offered Dwain anything more than my friendship. I thought once that we might be able to find some common ground on which to base a marriage, but fortunately I realized my mistake in time."

She stared at him, remembering Dwain's sad voice as he'd spoken so hesitantly about love. Suddenly she understood why he'd pressed so hard on their engagement, why he'd never wanted children. Dwain was a little boy who wanted her to love him and only him. Remorse gripped her as she considered this new facet of his character.

"Perhaps if you'd given him a chance, Dwain could have been talked around to parenthood," Jake muttered rudely, breaking into her thoughts. "A few other gowns like that one and he'd have come 'round, I'm sure."

Sasha stared at the strange tightness on his face. His eyes glittered angrily. "If you're trying to come up with a nepenthe that will wipe my mind totally clear of tonight," she gasped, "you have certainly done it."

"Oh, forget the stupid word games, for once," he rasped angrily. "How could you even think you wanted to have a child so badly you were willing to marry that—" he jerked a thumb over his shoulder "—creep, just to get pregnant?" He shook his head. "Even here in the backwoods, the choice of father material has got to be better than him."

Sasha held her temper in check and counted to five. But the Big and Little Dippers were still in the same positions in the summer night sky so she counted again. No change.

"I've already said I have no intention of marrying Dwain," she stated clearly, her voice ringing through the still night air. "I have not now, nor will I ever, sleep with any man just to have a child. There are other, better ways."

Now Jake was frowning. She could see the thoughts mirrored on his face in the growing light. Other, *better* ways? She knew exactly what he was thinking. If that wasn't just like a man!

"Just what *other, better ways* did you have in mind?" he challenged.

"Well, things like…artificial insemination," she answered readily. "That doesn't involve disgusting incidents like what just about happened here tonight. It's clean and sterile and I can still have a baby."

She watched Jake's dark head jerk as the sound of crickets chirping floated toward them from the nearby river.

"Clean and sterile?" He shook his black head scornfully.

"Lady, babies are supposed to come from the love of two people for each other and love is anything but sterile."

Sasha felt silly talking about it with him when he so obviously didn't want to see her point of view.

"I think you're being deliberately obtuse. I meant that the procedure doesn't involve people who have children as a result of bad situations like tonight."

Jake nodded bleakly. "It also doesn't involve anyone else to help you with night feedings and changing diapers and sickness and expenses or any of the other wonders children bring." He glared at her, his face tight with anger as he leaned nearer her longue. "Are you naturally this crazy or do you have to work at it?" he demanded.

"There is nothing crazy about wanting a child," she protested. "It's a perfectly natural, healthy response. Why shouldn't I have a child?"

"Because a child needs two parents if at all possible. Why do you think God designed it so that it takes two people to make a child? A baby needs all the attention and love and care it can get and one parent can't possibly do justice to the position. I should know," he muttered defensively.

"I'm not stupid, I know it will be tough." Sasha ignored his snide tone. She didn't really expect anyone else to understand this need she felt to make something wonderful out of her life.

"You have no idea at all," he told her ruefully. "No possible conception of what it will be like. Most people don't until it's too late and that darling little baby grows up into a whining two-year-old or a demanding five-year-old that can't be hushed with a bottle and changed diaper anymore. You think because you baby-sat for a while, that you can take on a child full-time?" He snorted derisively. "You won't be able to give it back, you know."

His voice grated on her nerves and Sasha just wanted him to stop ruining her dream. It had seemed so right, so good, to think of raising a child and now he was making it seem like she would be shortchanging her own child.

"Everything worthwhile has a price," she reminded him. She kept her voice low. "You wouldn't trade Cody for anything, would you?"

He sighed. "Of course not. But I sure as heck would give a lot to give him back his mother. She gave him things that I can't and never will be able to. That's the way families work—one parent complements the other."

A brooding silence hung between them that Sasha was loathe to break. Once more she had trod where angels feared to tread and broken the friendly banter they had so carefully built up over the past weeks.

Jake Windsor was sitting on her patio, silently contemplating the loss of his child's mother because of her foolish demands. It wasn't right. But how could she expect him to understand this need she had for a child of her own?

She leaned forward to press her hand on his shoulder. "I'm sorry, Jake. Really I am. I never meant to make you think that I don't understand the seriousness of having a child who is wholly dependent on you for its well-being." Sasha could feel the rough cotton fabric beneath her fingers as she moved her hand down his arm. Her fingers laced through his automatically, as if drawn there to give and receive comfort.

"I know that you wish your wife was here. I know that you love Cody and want the best of everything for him. Can't you understand that I want to feel those same feelings? That I want to have someone of my own to love?"

Her voice died away in the stillness as Sasha realized exactly what she had said. She'd admitted that she was lonely and alone in a world where love was the magic password to happiness. And she had admitted it to a single man who had rescued her from the clutches of a drunk in the middle of the night. A man who had told her many times that he had no desire for a wife or a mother for Cody. Sasha held her breath.

Please, please, don't let him take that the wrong way, she prayed. *Don't let him know that I'd give anything to have Cody for a son, and his father for a help-mate.*

Finally he looked up, his face drawn and haggard. He freed her fingers and moved back from her intent look.

"Find some nice guy and get married," he told her softly. "Then you can have as many children as you want. At least they'll have both parents."

She could feel the wall coming up between them brick by impenetrable brick. It was stupid and totally unnecessary and she wasn't going back to being the outsider. Whether Jake Windsor liked it or not, he was going to hear her side of this argument.

"And what happens if this nice guy takes a hike, or decides I don't turn him on anymore? What do I do then, Jake?"

His eyes glimmered briefly with a spark of life.

"I hardly think you're in much danger of the second," he muttered through clenched teeth. His eyes swept over her tumbled hair, clear face, long neck and well-covered body. "Not much danger at all. And your children will still have two parents even if he's not there at the moment."

Temper soared as she watched him withdraw inside himself. "I had two parents," she muttered finally, unable to stem the bitter flow of words. "I had a father and a mother in my home from the day I was born. That didn't guarantee me any kind of childhood happiness."

Jake's lean face rose to meet hers, his gray eyes startled.

"They fought continuously, Jake. About everything. I thought it was my fault. I was the oldest, therefore I should be the peacemaker, the good little girl who kept everything and everyone on an even keel. Maybe, I thought, maybe if I was very very good they would stop fighting and we kids would be safe. Loved. Cared for.'' She felt him take her hand once more, but she didn't—couldn't—stop speaking.

"It didn't work. Nothing I did was ever good enough to keep those two from fighting. Not cooking the meals, not cleaning my room, not getting good marks. Nothing."

Tears were rolling down her face, Sasha realized. Damn. She hadn't shed a tear for that sad, scared little girl in a long time. She dashed them away angrily and yanked her hand from his.

"Don't talk to me about two parent families," she snapped. "One or two parents, adopted or natural children, it doesn't make any difference if love is there." She glared at Jake fiercely. "I intend to love my child and to do the best for him no matter what it costs me. Children's needs come first. Always."

She stood then, dragging the heavy robe more closely around her.

"Be happy," she ordered in a no-nonsense tone. "Be very happy that your wife left Cody in your strong, capable hands. Deep down you have his best interests at heart more than anyone else he'll meet for many years to come. As his parent it's your responsibility to make sure he grows up knowing you love him."

She stopped for a moment, drawing in a long breath as she stared down at his amazed face.

"There are no guarantees in this life," she whispered. "And if you sit around waiting for them, you'll miss out. I don't intend to do that." She cleared her throat. "Cody is the best thing that could have happened to you even though you won't admit it."

She could see that he was thinking about her words, drawing them inside to roll over in his mind. Good! She moved slowly toward the back door and when she was there, turned to face him as he stood tall and strong.

"I just have one other thing to add."

He straightened, shoving his hands into his black cutoff shorts. His eyes glittered with frustration.

"Don't you ever give up?" he muttered.

Sasha's thudding heart noted the thick, strong muscles of his hairy legs, the narrow cut of his foot in the sneakers. She swallowed the tingle of desire that rippled through her body and stared straight into his gray eyes.

"Not when it's important. And this is the most important thing there is. Your son is probably the one person who has kept you going these past few years. Why do you want to deny me the same wonderful experience of knowing my own child?"

Jake watched her walk into the house, her words ringing through his head as he gazed around in the dawning light. He heard the bolt slide home and then waited for a light to come on.

Eventually he realized that she had gone to bed without turning on any lamps. Feeling like a burglar, he left her darkened yard, stepping out onto the brightly lit street as a bird chirped over his head.

It had been a night of revelations. His mind vividly recalled her lush, exotic body outlined in the thin nightdress, the way she had shuddered and huddled against him in her shock, the vehement fashion in which she had argued her case, and the haunting questions she had demanded he answer.

She would make a wonderful mother, Jake acknowledged. She was full of care and concern and fun and laughter; all the things a child would need to get through a lifetime. Sasha Lambert had strength and spirit and vitality enough to take on the challenge of a child with joy and wonder. And that child would have a mother to envy, someone dedicated to its well-being.

Then why, he asked himself angrily, did the thought of her giving birth to the child of some other man, bother him so much?

Because there was no way she should do it all alone, his mind answered. No way he would believe that anyone should have to handle the terrible aloneness that fell after your child had gone to bed, when there was no one to talk to about the day, the things he'd done, the jokes he'd told, the way he'd giggled when you tickled his bare feet. All the little things that made having a child so much more precious because you shared them with someone you loved.

And who would be there to hold her hand when that child left home for school and then college? Who would she focus on then? If only Sasha could see there was so much more to it than cuddling a cute little baby.

Jake strode past Old Man Handers and his dog with a wave and a muttered greeting, concentrating on the roiling emotions within.

Why was it, he asked himself angrily, that Sasha Lambert could always get him in this ridiculous tizzy?

The envelope from the clinic was full of information about the insemination process and long white legal sheets that needed filling out. Sasha had managed to answer most of the questions quite well, but this last one had her stumped.

"What does the future look like to you once Baby arrives? Please discuss at length."

These people weren't going to settle for "great" or "wonderful." They wanted specifics that showed she had put time and effort into planning the future.

Sasha chewed on the pencil tip as she thought about having that tiny form growing inside her. She glanced at the Lamaze books lying nearby and tried to imagine the miracle of giving birth. Her eyes feasted on the pictures of LaLeche mothers nursing their infants. Both mother and child glowed with blissful happiness.

A hard rapping on the screen door jolted her from the

fussy dream and back to reality. Her eyes gaped at Jake
Windsor's rain-coated figure as he strode through the door.

"What in the—"

He interrupted her without apology. "Rachel Andrews
has been rushed to Billings for surgery. Her husband says
his mother will be here tomorrow morning to look after the
baby. I thought maybe, since you're so fond of children,
you could take him tonight. I've got the other kids in the
car. I'll parcel them out around town for tonight. Formula's
in the bag." The words flowed out in a rush, leaving her
no time to respond before he set the carrier on the floor
and strode back out the door. Seconds later he was back.

"Diapers," he grunted, plopping a bag down on the
floor.

"Look, Jake, I don't think I can baby-sit tonight. I've
got some..." Sasha's voice trailed away as he glanced at
the sheaf of papers covering the kitchen table. She watched
the corners of his mouth tip down as he read the heading
on each. His eyes flashed with some unspoken remark she
was glad went unsaid.

"The Lord works in mysterious ways, Sasha. Looks like
he's answered your prayers for a baby." His voice was hard
and cold, full of disdain. One long finger flicked the corner
of the envelope. "Even if it's just temporarily. Tim here,
is just two months old. And he needs you. I reckon he
won't squawk too much at being a guinea pig for your little
plan." He grinned facetiously. "I'll be back in an hour to
check up on you. Just in case you flunk the test."

Baby Tim chose that moment to express his disgust with
the whole operation. His voice was not a gentle coo of
dismay but a loud, raucous squall that demanded immediate
satisfaction.

Sasha bent over the carrier and unfolded the tiny bundle.
And although his big blue eyes opened to stare at her,
Tim's tiny rosebud mouth did not shut. Not once. Instead

he protested even more vigorously, jabbing at her torso with his poky arms and feet.

"My signal to go," Jake teased. "And remember. Babies are supposed to be fun!"

With a chuckle he was out the door before Sasha could form the words that would tell him precisely what she thought of his arrangements.

"Okay, Tim. Let's check your diaper." She laid him out on the bathroom counter and pulled away the plastic tabs. Sure enough, the wad of tissue was soaked. But she had forgotten that diaper bag in the kitchen.

Now what?

Sasha glanced around the tiny bathroom, trying to decide her next step. Her eyes flew back to her tiny charge when a warm wet substance soaked through the thin fabric of her shirt. She grimaced in disgust.

"You're supposed to wait until I get the diaper on before you do that," she told him sadly. Tim burst out bawling again.

"All right. All right! I'll get another diaper." She whipped one of her favorite white monogrammed towels off the rack and swathed it around his little hips, wondering why she had chosen today to change to her best linens.

The bag was sitting where Jake had left it and Sasha snatched out one of the thick white diapers. Tim hadn't stopped screaming and it didn't help her nerves one bit as she fumbled with the plastic sticky tabs. Unfortunately they were the type that once stuck, stayed stuck. The garment bagged around his little tummy, lopsidedly hugging one leg.

"I'm sorry, kid, but this is gonna have to do. I'm a little out of practice. As far as I can see, Jake only brought four of these and we might have a long night ahead."

Tim stared at her for one infinitesimal second before his mouth opened again and he began that loud shriek of distress that set her teeth rattling. As Sasha bent to search for a bottle, she heard the rattle of papers. She straightened quickly and noticed his baby hand clutching one sheet, scrunching it up in his tiny fingers.

"Give it to me, Tim. That's a good boy. Come on, let go." With every prying movement, Tim's voice increased by several decibels.

When at last she had the paper free, Sasha glanced at it with a frown. He would have to take the one she was working on, the one about the future. And tear the corner to shreds, she noticed regretfully.

"Come on, fella. Let's get some dinner into you and then maybe you'll sleep." He bellowed even louder. "Whatever you say," she muttered, anxiously slipping the bottle into the microwave.

If she could just get his bottle warm enough to stop that incessant wailing her headache might cure itself. It was either that or put him in a soundproof room. Now there was an idea!

Sasha lifted the bottle from the microwave and tested a bit on her arm. Good—just right. She tipped Tim gently from her shoulder and tried to slip the nipple into his mouth. He sucked hard several times and then burst into fresh wails of distress.

"Look, kid. If you want something to eat you've got to get this thing into your mouth. Try again." Well, she was willing but Tim wasn't. Instead his little arms fluttered about and his tiny face turned an even darker shade of red.

Sasha walked with him into the living room and gently laid him on the sofa with pillows tucked around. Straightening, she tipped the bottle up for a closer look as her fingers gently squeezed the pliable plastic bag.

"Everything looks okay. The nipple's not plugged, Timothy, and the temperature is just...ooooooooooooh!" Baby formula, warm and wet, washed over her hair, face, neck and shoulders as the thin plastic liner suddenly gave way.

Tim gurgled happily, waving his little arms with exhilaration. He, it seemed, was enjoying himself.

"Well," she muttered in frustration, "at least one of us is having fun." Sasha raced to the kitchen to grab a cloth and then ran back before little Tim took a flying leap off the sofa onto the floor. She eyed the mother and child book and then shook her head.

No point in trying to read up on it now, she told herself, wiping off as much of the sticky white substance as she could reach. "You've just got to go with what you know." Which seemed to be the signal for the baby to renew its cries of frustration.

"I am going to personally search you out, Jake Windsor, and when I do, you're going to pay, very dearly, for this." Tim stared up at her for a moment before resuming that deafening squall in her left ear.

Sasha patted his back, rubbed his tummy, tickled his feet, walked him, jiggled him and sang to him. None of which seemed to work.

"Okay, bucko. We'll try the bottle thing again. But I'm warning you. It's going to take a while. I'm heating it the old-fashioned way and that could take some time."

It took forever for the kettle to boil and ages for the milk to heat. And the entire time Baby Timothy bawled.

It's not normal, her subconscious chided. *Can't you tell when a baby cries too much, oh, great mother to be. He'll get sick and then you'll be in trouble.*

"Just shut up, will you," Sasha muttered.

"I haven't said anything yet," Jake informed her, startling Sasha so badly she almost dropped the child. The two teaspoons of formula that Tim had swallowed before the bottle disintegrated came up all over her shoulder. There wasn't anything to do but groan. What a mess!

"And I only came because I thought you might like some help. The other kids are all settled."

"Now see what you've done," she growled, glaring at

him as she patted the baby. "You've scared the daylights out of him, too."

Carefully she set the baby on her tummy, face first, and attempted to encourage him to suck on the now tepid bottle.

"Why are you trying to feed him like that?" Jake inquired meekly. She could see the laughter begging to be released.

"I thought if he didn't see my face, he'd think I was his mother," Sasha told him, feeling ridiculously out of place.

"Oh."

They sat silently as Tim clamped his mouth around the bottle and drank. For the first time in eons, silence reigned. Sasha reveled in it as she watched him drink.

"I haven't done all that badly," she told Jake smugly in a proud, self-righteous tone as he sank down opposite her on the purple masterpiece. "At least I'm still relatively clean below my waist and…"

She stopped when Jake began shaking his head, face wreathed in a wide-toothed grin.

"Um, I don't think so," he murmured. She watched him try to get that smart-aleck grin under control. "There seems to be some problem with that diaper."

Sasha looked down, half afraid of what she would see. As she did, a pungent odor wafted upward, graphically explaining her predicament.

"Oh, no," she wailed softly. "Not on my new jeans."

He grinned. "They'll wash."

Sasha glared at him as she stood gingerly to her feet, dish towel at the ready. "They're white," she snapped. "Or they were. Now they're…" Her voice trailed away disconsolately as she walked on eggs to the bathroom, holding a now silent Tim away from her.

"Now they're not so white," he offered, trailing behind her. "That's the way it is with kids. You've just got to make some sacrifices."

Sasha filled the sink as she bit down hard on her tongue.

There was no way she was going to start a fight now. She had something to prove and for once, Jake Windsor was going to see just how wrong he was about her.

"Come on, baby," she said soothingly to the fretting child as she cleaned and then bathed him. "Let's get you nice and dry for beddy." Drying, powdering, dressing. It was all so special, especially now that Timmy had stopped wailing.

"There we go. Now go see Uncle Jake, honey." She slid the drowsy child into his arms and whispered, "Your turn, hotshot."

His hands closed willingly around the child but as he cradled the little boy, Timothy went off into fresh paroxysms of crying.

Jake frowned.

"Something sure smells funny," he muttered. His gray eyes searched hers. "Do you think he could be dirty again?"

Sasha flushed bright red and looked down at the floor.

"I think it could be me. Either my shirt or my hair or my jeans. Take your pick." She pushed him through the door and locked it. "You can handle one little baby, can't you?" she called through the door. "I need to have a long hot soak." She heard his muffled laughter rumbling over Tim's wails.

"Just think, Sasha. All this, and more, could be yours on a permanent basis." She swallowed her reply with difficulty and heard his whispered tone. "Daunting, isn't it?"

She yanked open the door and faced him down.

"Yes, it's daunting. It's dirty, hard, frustrating work. But no matter how hard it gets, I'm still going to want a child."

"But you were just complaining about ruining your jeans." Jake spluttered, a frown rippling his forehead. "I thought…"

She nodded. "You thought if I saw how bad it could be, I'd give up on my idea. Well, I'm not giving up. Not ever.

I can change my jeans or buy a new pair. If I'd known I was going to be baby-sitting, I'd have worn something else.'' Sasha narrowed her gaze and peered into his eyes. ''You're not going to change my mind, Jake. I am going to have a baby.''

His eyes never left hers, searching the green depths for an answer Sasha didn't have. Finally he turned to go.

''Have your bath,'' he muttered. ''I'll hand him over when you're ready.'' He shook his head in frustration. ''So blasted stubborn,'' he mumbled.

Forty-five minutes later, Sasha emerged from her room refreshed and clean. She felt invigorated, ready to tackle little Timothy and his caretaker.

''Time for the A-team...'' Her voice died away. Jake sprawled huddled in her purple armchair, head down with his chin resting on his chest and snoring gently. Sasha studied every detail of his handsome face from the thick swath of black lashes lying against his flushed cheeks to the long, straight nose and the wide full lips. Beside him, Timothy lay snuggled in one arm, his tiny chest moving rhythmically with each breath.

Her heart fluttered with the rightness of the picture. This was what she wanted, her mind whispered. A husband holding their child close. A man who wouldn't be afraid to shoulder some of the burden of child-rearing because he loved both the child and his mother. The picture pulled away and then focused once more with a sharpness and clarity that wouldn't be denied.

What Sasha Lambert wanted most in her life was this husband and his child. Deidre was right, she wasn't immune. She wanted to be loved by Jake Windsor every bit as much as she wanted to love him back.

It wasn't sensible to fall in love with your minister. And it certainly wasn't intelligent to expect a man who, like Jake, had been through hell, to forget all that just because she'd come along. But wasn't his love worth fighting for, worth working toward?

Carefully, quietly, she tiptoed backward into the kitchen and as silently as possible slid all the papers from the clinic back into the envelope. Without a backward look, she dropped them into a drawer and slid it gently closed.

A baby of her own was a dream she could put on hold. For now. But her feelings for Jake were new and untried. She couldn't give up on him. Not just yet. Not before she had exhausted every chance.

He was attracted to her, she knew that. His eyes had gleamed with an inner light that Sasha felt sure meant he had noticed her. He had teased and tormented and cajoled her for weeks now while that spark of electricity sizzled between them. Surely he felt something?

Sasha ignored the cautionary voice in her head and smiled. She would wait him out. Until he made the first move, anyway. Her head seemed somehow clearer as she came to the decision. As if that family picture she had tried to visualize for so long was finally complete when she added Jake and Cody.

"Jake," she murmured, wiggling his shoulder gently. "Jake?" His wide gray eyes blinked open as she picked up Timothy and cradled him in her arms. "I'll take over now. You go on home. You're exhausted."

She heard the tenderness in her own tones and smiled. So this was what loving felt like—wonderful!

"Are you sure you won't need help with him?" Jake towered over her seated figure, his voice husky, full of puzzled concern. "I thought…"

"Little Tim and I are going to be just fine," she assured him softly. "You go and get some sleep." As she cradled the tiny body, Sasha marveled at how right it felt. Warm and snug and, well, wonderful.

Jake sauntered to the door, shaking his head and muttering.

"First she wants him, then she doesn't, then she does. I don't get it." His eyes skimmed the bare tabletop and then flew to search hers for an answer. "You're really determined to do this," he asked quietly.

Sasha nodded. "Yes." She didn't enlighten him any further.

As he stood there staring at her, a wide grin flashed out, creasing his face into a series of smiles.

"Well, at least when you diaper your own kid backward, I'll be around to help out," he chuckled, glancing at Timothy's bottom. "All you have to do is call. After all, that's what friends are for."

Sasha watched him walk away with a pain in her heart. She didn't want him as just a friend. She wanted oh, so much more than that.

But, for now, she'd take what she could get.

Chapter Seven

Sasha whistled through her teeth as she finished the last of the stars on top of the character cake she had promised Cody would be at his birthday party tomorrow.

Truth to tell, she intended to use the cake as an excuse to stop by to see how things were going. Jake had said very little when she'd spoken to him on the phone this morning, but then the tension in his voice could have been caused by her flippant replies to his questions.

"Tim and I did just fine," she'd answered for the tenth time. "His grandmother showed up about eight and she took him back home. No problems."

"And have you changed your mind yet again?" he'd demanded. "You can still back out, you know."

Sasha had choked back her tears and kept her voice firm. "I have no intention of backing out. Ever. That was the most wonderful experience I could have had. Great preparation for when I have my own child."

"Sasha, one night isn't a whole lifetime. It takes all your stamina and—"

She cut off his frustrated voice.

"Look, we're never going to agree on my right to have a baby, but it is my decision. Let's call a truce. Okay?"

"Fine," he agreed grumpily. "I won't bring the subject up again unless you do first." Sasha had heaved a sigh of relief and quietly listened to his plans for Cody's birthday, ignoring the stab of regret in her heart.

Now her lips thinned as she remembered her first visitor this morning. Dwain's mother had ostensibly come to apologize for her son's behavior. The words had been faltering and red-faced but probably sincere. Apparently Dwain had been ashamed enough to admit to his whining parent that he'd exercised an attack of bravado in response to something he'd overheard. Something that had to do with her and the town's new minister. Sasha had no doubt the woman standing in front of her was his source of this malicious gossip.

"You seem to think I'm some sort of scarlet woman. I assure you that I have neither the time nor the inclination," Sasha had scoffed, frowning as she watched the fleshy face glower back. "The only reason I can't marry your son is because I don't love him, not because I'm involved with someone else." It had been the bald truth and Sasha had winced as she said it.

"I'm sorry," she'd murmured, softening just a bit. "I tried, I really did. But he and I are not right for each other and I can't pretend anymore."

"I knew *that* all along," his mother had agreed loudly. "And now Dwain knows it, too. It's just as well really. My son isn't the sort of man who would want his fiancée out with the preacher, necking in the woods. Why, the whole town is talking. It's scandalous!"

Sasha was furious. She glared at the cantankerous old woman with darkened eyes.

"Are you so sure it was me?" she'd demanded, watching the sagging face and watery blue eyes for some sign of prevarication.

"Tall and dark, they said. And wearing one of those long skirts, almost to the ground, like you often wear." The self-righteous face reddened. "The couple were hugging. And to think that you and my son were practically engaged!" She shook her head. "I've already been to see the reverend and given him a piece of my mind." She sniffed. "He denied it, too."

"Of course he did." Sasha kept her voice very calm and even, although her cheeks were hot with temper. "I haven't been out walking in the woods with anyone lately. And the only person I can think of tall enough to be mistaken for me is Tara Langot. Since she's supposed to be away on a shoot right now, I don't think it would be her."

Jealousy, pure and green, rolled through her system, its fangs biting deep into her heart. Tara was the local beauty who had left home to make a name for herself in the fashion industry. The resemblance ended with their height. Tara always had swarms of elegantly handsome men waiting to take her out. She had beauty and money and brains. Comparing them, Sasha decided, was ludicrous.

"My son is too good for you, Sasha Lambert. Far too good. He needs his mother to watch out for his interests, and make no mistake, I intend to watch you very carefully."

"Dwain is a grown man," Sasha murmured thoughtfully, thinking about his halting words from the night before and wondering if it was his need to be loved that had drawn her to him in the first place.

"Maybe what your son really needs is someone who will simply love him for himself." She studied the angry face in front of her. "And someone he feels free to love back," she added. "No strings attached."

Dwain's mother had glared at her, her mouth a thin straight line that barely parted to issue her last punch.

"He doesn't need anyone else," she'd decreed forcefully. Her eyes were like chips of hardened stone. "My

Dwain has his mother to care for him.'' The angry woman had sailed out of the door like a battleship setting sail, muttering epithets as she went.

"I know,'' Sasha thought, grimacing at the distasteful scene. "Perhaps that's the problem.''

She didn't have time to dwell on it anymore just then because Mrs. Bratley came bursting into the store asking for a small box of the specialty chocolates.

"I thought they would be a great homecoming gift for my daughter-in-law. New baby, you know, and since she's not breast feeding, I know she'd just love a few bonbons.''

Sasha dutifully asked all the appropriate questions and admired the sheaf of snaps Vera had unfolded inside her wallet, while skillfully packing the delicate confections into the gold foil box.

"By the way, dear, I saw you and the pastor out walking again last evening. Do you think it's a good idea to spend so much time alone in his company? After all, he is still recovering from his wife's death, you know.''

"Yes, actually I do know, Vera,'' she muttered with an edge to her voice. "But thank you for telling me. And just for the record, it wasn't me out there. I was home baking a cake.''

She refused to divulge the owner of the cake, choosing instead to continue piping on the black railroad tracks that ran around the base of the white cardboard circle she had used to display Cody's cake.

"Oh.'' Vera's white forehead creased in dismay. "But I was sure that floppy red hat was yours.'' She smiled happily. "Oh, well, that's fine then.'' She scurried from the store like a wren busily gathering her supplies into the capacious shopping bag she always carried.

Sasha grimaced as another wave of annoyance surged through her. Everyone seemed to think it was perfectly all right that their new minister was out walking at night with some woman, as long as it wasn't her! Well, she wanted to know who it was and she wanted to know now.

With more force than strictly necessary she pressed the plastic circus top into place and lined the tracks with the railroad cars. The little flag with "Happy Birthday Cody" printed across it flew at just the right angle from the big top. Sasha stood back to admire the effect and was just congratulating herself when the tiny silver bell above the door rang once more.

"What now?" she wondered, unscrewing the metal tip from her icing bag.

"Now that's what I call a birthday cake." Jake Windsor whistled out loud. "Very nice."

"Thank you." She kept her tone cool and controlled, her head downbent as she gathered her equipment to take to the sink for washing. "Is there something I can get for you?"

When she looked up, his gray eyes were glinting silver sparks of amusement at her. He had leaned his lanky body against her counter and was smiling the self-satisfied smile of a man who had a secret.

"Yes, please. I'd like six of those helium balloons. All colors. Some goodie bags and stuff to go in them, party hats and that little birthday sign in the window."

She gathered everything together without a word, packing everything but the balloons in a big plastic bag.

"What's the bell for?" he asked, watching her tie a tinkling silver bell at the bottom of each balloon's ribbon.

"Keeps them from lifting off when you don't want them to," she murmured.

"Oh."

"Anything else?"

"Yes. I want six of each of these, although I have no idea what they are aside from some type of food, and of course, the shoelaces. I suggested the grocery store for those but Cody insisted they were kept here."

She took the list from his hand and glanced down at it.

"Cherry bellers, plum sours, peach slices, lemon zingers, watermelon fuzzies and red shoelaces." She glanced up. "He means licorice shoelaces, not real ones." With nimble fingers she plucked the long stringy items from the jar and held them up for display.

"He's going to get everyone sick if they eat all this stuff at the party. Don't give it to them until they leave at the end."

Sasha carried the candy in her store purely as a favor to the local kids who didn't have a huge selection of penny candy to choose from. When one container ran out, she'd order a new one for them to try. At Halloween she gave them out as treats.

Swiftly she counted out the required amount, adding an extra one in each case.

"Hey, that's seven." Jake was frowning at her. "Cody's not eating that junk. Not after cake and hot dogs and all the rest."

"It's not for him. It's for an extra kid who sometimes wasn't invited and shows up anyway." She watched his gray eyes widen in shock.

"You mean, more than six might be there?"

She nodded. "Someone's brother or sister is liable to show up. Better safe than sorry."

"Oh, Lord, why did I ever let myself get talked into this," he groaned, tugging on the mussed black strands that fell across one eye. The sunny look had completely left his craggy features.

"I'm sure you'll manage just fine. Why don't you ask the woman you've been out walking with to help?" It slipped out without warning and Sasha immediately wished it unsaid. Jake looked amused.

"Janice? I don't think so." He shook his dark head firmly. "She's not much better than I am with hordes of children, and anyway, she hates to get her fingernails dirty." The imparting of that information seemed to restore his good humor, although it did nothing at all for Sasha's.

So, her name was Janice. Sasha whipped the bags into the large carrying sack and passed it across to him.

"Anything else?" she muttered, her face warm with embarrassment.

"Yes." His tone surprised her. "I'm going to try one of those."

Sasha stared at him, eyes widening at the silly grin on his face. She gaped as he picked up the tongs and took out one of the sour gumballs.

"You won't like it," she warned him. "It's grape."

"I love grape bubblegum," he answered, sliding the huge ball around in his mouth. "It's my favorite."

She watched as he chewed slowly, the long stringy pieces sticking to his teeth and seeming to weld his jaw shut. Her good humor suddenly reasserted itself as he finally rolled the entire mess into a tissue.

"I guess I'm out of practice," he told her. "I'd better take one home and try again."

"You'd better clean up before you go." She grinned, handing him a mirror and a wet wipe. "Otherwise your mommy won't let you in the door."

"There's only Janice home right now and she's devoted to the soaps. I don't think she'd notice if my hair was green." He grinned at her. "My sister has a thing for all those passion flicks. Unfortunately, her daughter is learning the same habit."

Sasha did a second take. Sister? Daughter? She forced the scream of frustration back down her throat.

"Is your sister staying long?" Calm soothing breaths, she ordered her racing heart. Relax.

His eyes sparkled at her as if he had seen inside to the curiosity that plagued her in regard to his houseguest. Sasha ignored his smirk and leaned over to pick up the bits of packaging he'd dropped.

Unfortunately, Jake chose that precise moment to do exactly the same thing and whacked her forehead with his own hard head.

"Ow! Oh, sorry." She straightened, holding a hand to her temple. "I didn't realize…"

"No, it's my fault," he assured her. His white teeth flashed in the sunlight coming through the window. "I shouldn't have dropped it in the first place."

His long forefinger brushed over her temple, sending a wave of sensation through her body. "Are you okay? No serious damage?" His mouth brushed ever so softly over her forehead, skimming across, leaving a trail of fire in its wake.

None that's visible, Sasha thought, and tried to school her features into an uncaring mask when the truth was that this man aroused more naughty desires in her than anyone she had ever met.

She tried not to pull away as his hand smoothed her bangs back and the gray eyes searched for a bruise.

"I hit you pretty hard." He smiled sympathetically. "It must hurt like the dickens."

Sasha could not force her eyes away from his probing glance.

"I'll be fine," she whispered, standing still and taut under his gently ministering hand. His fingers didn't stop their gentle caress and not for the life of her could Sasha move away from that mesmerizing touch.

She didn't want it to end. She realized with startled perception that she wanted this closeness, this strange heart-stopping awareness to go on and on. She wanted him to slide his long lean hands down her shoulders and arms and pull her against him. She wanted…

"Sasha?" His softly enquiring voice broke her reverie.

"Yes."

"Are you sure you're all right? You look a little dazed."

She decided he was a master of understatement.

"You haven't asked how I am." The teasing note in his voice caused her to glance at him suspiciously.

"Well? How are you?"

"It hurts." He pointed to the area above his left eyebrow.

"And?" She wasn't going into this without a little more information, Sasha decided. He was teasing her, playing a coquettish game that was totally out of character for the man who claimed to want no truck with women.

"I think it's part of the mothering thing to kiss and make it better." He grinned. "You can practice on me if you want."

Obediently Sasha leaned forward and pressed her lips against his brow with a feather-light touch before moving back. "Better?"

"Amazing." He grinned. "The kids really have something this time. A kiss actually does make it feel better." The gray eyes were darkly provocative. "Think how much better I'd feel if—"

Sasha interrupted him with a shake of her head.

"Don't go there," she told him brusquely. "I don't want to be accused of being a man-hunting female again, just looking to take over you and your son."

His craggy face flushed a dull red.

"I shouldn't have said that," he admitted softly. "You're not the type to horn in where you're not wanted." His speculative eyes moved over her white sundress and flat sandals. "I know now that you are the type of woman who gives and gives without asking for anything. I just want to say thank-you for helping with Cody's party. You are making it very special for him, and I appreciate it."

The tension was thick between them. That wasn't bad, it was just very intense and Sasha needed time to think it through.

"Hey," she joked, playfully punching him in the shoulder. "Don't make me out to be Mother Teresa. I still expect to be paid for that." She motioned to the bag of candy on the counter and grinned up at him. "And I am not organizing games for your party. That's your job."

He laughed and shook his head. "No, I don't expect you to help. But we do want you to come. Both of us. Cody sent a special invitation."

Sasha studied the laboriously printed card with interest before glancing up to meet his penetrating gray stare. "Are you sure?"

The Reverend Jacob Windsor winked. Sasha was positive she saw it, and the twinkle sparkling in the depth of his eyes only confirmed her first assessment.

"I don't think..." She hesitated. Discretion was highly underrated, she decided. It would have been better to have ignored this man right from day one. Better for her thudding heart, anyway.

"Aw, come on. It'll be a riot." He grinned down at her.

Sasha nodded sagely. "Exactly what I was thinking."

He tipped his head to one side and considered her through narrowed eyes.

"This was your advice, remember? Don't you want to see the monster you've created?"

"My..." Sasha laughed. "What an intriguing invitation. All right, I'll be there." He paid her and turned to leave.

"Oh, and make sure you bring along a bathing suit," he ordered, turning back. "You'll need it."

"A swimsuit? Why do I need—"

But he was gone, whistling out the door before she could ask anything more.

Now what in the world had he planned that included water? Sasha wondered, fear and trepidation filling her mind. Surely he didn't intend to take seven preschoolers to the creek? All by himself?

Sasha glanced up at the tall, smugly grinning father who lounged lazily beside her and stated the obvious. "This was a fantastic idea."

Seven children whooped and hollered around the Windsors' backyard, vying for position and a turn on the makeshift water slide Jake had erected. Everyone was drenched, including the adults, but no one cared.

"Yeah, I thought so, too." He beamed smugly. "Actually, Cody gave me the idea. He said he wanted to go to a water slide in the city." His eyes gently mocked her. "The mere thought of driving for two hours with those kids in the car made me decide we could improvise. Seems to be working."

Sasha would have agreed but a flood of water cascaded over her at that precise moment, preventing any response.

"Cody," his father protested. "Put that thing down. You're drowning her."

Sasha heard Cody's chirpy little voice respond with glee. "I know. And now it's your turn."

"You did say you wanted him to behave like a normal six-year-old," he reminded her, wiping a hand across his face. "Is this normal?" He blinked down at her, his dark eyelashes spiky around those clear gray eyes.

Sasha grinned. "Very," she told him pertly, and grabbed the hose from Cody to turn it on him herself.

"Hey! I'm the host. It's not dignified—"

She never heard the rest as the cold stream of water caught him squarely in the face. She did hear his threat of reprisal. "That's it. This is war."

Giggling uncontrollably, Sasha immediately dropped the hose and raced for cover inside the house. The kitchen seemed the safest bet so she scurried in there and was calmly peering into the fridge when he surged in moments later.

"You can run but you can't hide," he threatened, advancing slowly over the cleanly polished linoleum. "It's payback time."

Sasha laughed nervously, glancing around surreptitiously.

"I was just cooling you off," she murmured in a sweet little-girl voice. "It's such a hot afternoon." She moved skittishly to one side. "I think I'll have some lemonade."

"Before or after I soak you?" he growled, wrapping his long brown fingers around her arm.

"You wouldn't really turn the garden hose on a guest, would you?" It was meant to cow him but there was no obvious effect, Sasha noticed. Jake merely grinned.

"That little shower you treated me to was gelid," he whispered, tugging her closer. "I always reciprocate a favor with a favor."

Sasha stared at him blankly. "'Gelid'?" He chose an odd time to take up their word war, she decided sourly.

"Extremely cold." The words barely left his lips before he'd scooped her into his arms and moved toward the door. "Your time is here," he growled into her ear. "Prepare for a shower colder than the Arctic ice floes."

"No, you can't. I'm allergic to cold. I didn't mean it. I'm sorry." Sasha struggled wildly, but his arms were like steel bands around her. She couldn't even hang on to her tormentor easily since he'd applied some type of oil that made his smooth skin slippery.

His hand was under her knees while his other arm cupped her waist, almost grazing the curve of her right breast. She could feel his chest hairs tickling her ribs and the scent of coconuts permeated the air around them. It was a good thing he carried her, Sasha decided, because her knees were limp as dishrags.

His face was only inches away from hers, grinning with victory as one piece of dark hair draped itself across his brow. He looked like a little boy, and he felt anything but!

"Please, Jake," she pleaded, shaken by her awareness of him. "I hate cold water. It gives me hives and I shiver for hours."

"Good." He grinned. "Then you'll know how I feel."

She brushed her hand across his gleaming shoulder, pressing gently against the bulge of muscle.

"But you're not cold," she objected. Her fingers pressed against his chest firmly. "You're not cold at all."

He'd stopped, Sasha realized. They were almost at the door but Jake was making no move to continue their trek through the back door. She glanced up at his face and tensed at the strange look she found there.

"No," he said quietly. "I'm not cold. Not in the least." His eyes were piercing in their scrutiny and they never wavered from their hold on hers. As if in slow motion, his head bent lower and lower until his face was mere centimeters from hers.

"In fact, I'm burning up." And indeed, his mouth, when it finally touched hers felt hot, like a touch of fire. "Kiss me, Sasha," he whispered, easing her legs to the floor as his arms wrapped themselves around her slim body.

"I will. I mean, I am." The words came out jerkily, on a half breath of desire.

His finger rose to trace the full sensuous tilt of her lower lip. "Like this."

The words were gossamer-soft in the quiet of the kitchen with the noise of laughing children just outside the door. She felt his mouth tease and caress hers, asking for a response that she couldn't stop even if she'd wanted to. And she didn't want it to stop. Not now. Not ever.

Jake's hands pulled her closer against his own lean form and she slipped her hands over the smooth golden skin of his back, delighting in the sensation of his body against hers.

His hair-roughened legs brushed against her starting those tingling ripples of excitement that were echoed in the tug of his mouth on hers. Her body felt vibrantly alive and she opened her lips, just a fraction, to taste his burning kiss.

His hands were smoothing over her back, past the strap of her swimsuit and down the line of her spine to her hips.

And everywhere his hands moved over her, her skin purred, like a cat rubbing itself against a human.

She groaned as his kiss deepened, drawing his questing tongue deeper inside, shifting against him more comfortably as his arms tightened around her. Now his mouth was moving, nibbling on the cord of her neck, leaving a trail of jingling sensations in its wake. This was what she'd thought of whenever she had considered lovemaking, Sasha realized. This craving for more and more of Jake's tender touch on her sensitive skin.

"I think you're the most gorgeous woman I have ever known," he murmured, his hands moving to encircle her waist. He nipped her ear and slid his mouth over her smooth forehead. "When you were created, everything was placed exactly right." His voice was so soft Sasha barely heard it.

But she did feel the burning touch of his finger as he brushed the underside of her breast. It was a sensation so exquisite that Sasha felt her knees buckle. And she would have fallen had he not been holding her.

She stared up into the strong lean face and felt her world drop silently to her feet.

She loved him! Sasha accepted it with amazement. She had allowed herself to fall in love with Jake Windsor, a man who was still grieving the loss of his wife. A man who made no bones about the fact that he had no intention of replacing his dead wife or Cody's mother anytime soon. A man with no place in his future for someone like her.

He needed female companionship, that was all. And she was handy. After Dwain's little contretemps, Jake probably thought she was fair game.

She was lost in her thoughts when his voice broke through her musings.

"It seems we have an audience."

Sasha turned to discover seven wide-eyed children staring at them as they dripped puddles of water onto the floor.

Their interested gazes took in the fact that Cody's father was holding a woman in his arms.

The door on the other side of the kitchen opened then and a tall, dark-haired woman peered in.

"Awfully quiet outside, Ja— Oh, I see." And then her stern, harsh features creased into a plethora of smiles. "Brother, dear," she crowed jubilantly. "Your timing sucks."

Jake released Sasha slowly and she simply stood there, transfixed. His sister had no such problem as she hustled the children outside.

"Come along, kids. We'll have the barbecue going shortly."

"Cody's dad was kissin' Miss Sasha!" a squeaky precocious announcement broke through the silence.

"Yes, I noticed, dear. Shall we make water balloons?" Sasha could hear the dry tones of amusement in the older woman's voice.

But their curiosity was not to be denied. "Why?"

A soft silence then and Sasha sought out Jake's dark brooding gaze.

"Because he wanted to, I expect," was the nonchalant reply. "Now come on, get the water hose going and we'll fill up these balloons."

It was enough to divert them and they barreled into the fun, virtually ignoring the pair in the kitchen.

"I'm sorry," Jake muttered brusquely, his eyes dull and void of the sparkling humor she had seen earlier.

Sasha flushed a dark red. She wasn't sorry, not in the least. Couldn't he see that they had something going just then? Something special and wonderful?

"It's all right. I have been kissed before, you know." She couldn't keep the tone of bitterness from her voice. His hand grasped her arm when she would have whirled out the door.

"I didn't mean for kissing you. I think we both know

that that was reciprocal." His face was shaded, his emotions hidden from her now as he shifted toward the counter. "I meant for embarrassing you. Those kids will blab to their parents and the whole town will be talking about it for the next week." He had flushed a dark red.

"There's nothing to talk about," Sasha declared bitterly. "Nothing at all."

"Sasha?" She turned back at the pleading tone in his voice. "I like you. You're smart and funny and you have a special rapport with Cody that I admire." He grinned self-deprecatingly but Sasha could see that he was backtracking. "I'm even half jealous, if you want to know the truth. I lost a lot of time we should have spent together when I left his care up to my mother."

She stood, silent, waiting.

"But I shouldn't have kissed you. I shouldn't have let you believe I felt something when we both know there can never be anything between us."

She fixed her eyes on the dimple in the corner of his mouth and forced herself to hear what he was saying.

"I'm the minister of this town, the spiritual confidant for my parishioners. And I have a young son to raise. I can't afford to let myself get involved again."

Sasha walked over to where he leaned on the counter and stared him straight in the eye.

"Can't or won't?" she demanded quietly. And then she did something she had never done before. She leaned forward and kissed an unsuspecting male for all she was worth. On the lips. Hard.

And for one infinite moment in time he responded.

But that was before he came to his senses and pressed her away from him.

"Don't," he half whispered. "Don't tempt me."

Sasha pretended she didn't hear it. Heartbroken, she wheeled away and was almost out the door before she turned back to stare at him.

"Don't worry about it. I have my own plans," she told him, drawing a modicum of panache from some unknown reserve. "I'll have to get to work on that right away." The words came as Sasha accepted that she was giving up on him, on building something wonderful between them.

He stared at her. "The artificial insemination?"

Sasha nodded.

"You see, Jake, the difference between us is that I know what I want from life and I'm not afraid to go after it until I get it." Her eyes roved slowly over his handsome face and tautly muscled body. She grimaced when he swerved his eyes away from her intense scrutiny, but continued anyway. "You won't even try."

The afternoon dragged for Sasha after that. She slipped on her shirt and shorts and helped Janice with the barbecue, slathering ketchup and mustard onto several dozen hot dogs as requested. Jake reappeared a little later, also dressed, and they spent the afternoon avoiding each other's eyes.

The children appeared to notice nothing amiss and there was great hilarity when Cody's cake finally made its debut. When the sparklers started the plastic table cloth on fire Bobby Bratley grabbed the hose and sprayed it out with quick-thinking deftness that surprised everyone.

"Nothing to it." He grinned proudly.

The towering pile of gifts was opened and Cody couldn't stop grinning at the array of toys that he received. Sasha slipped her own present off the pile and out of sight when the boy opened his father's gift of a train set.

"Dad! It's great. Thank you." Cody squeezed his father in a bear hug before dashing back to the box of cars and track. "Can we set it up now?"

"Well, I think we'd better wait till later. It takes a bit of time and we need a big board to put the track on."

She noted the look of satisfaction covering Jake's face.

"It used to be mine," he told his son softly. "Auntie Janice brought it with her when she came down."

"I promise, cross my heart—" he made the motion "—I'll be very, very careful with it." Cody hugged his father tightly.

"I was worried for a while, but I think those two might finally be working things out," Janice murmured from behind her. Sasha turned to face the austere woman who had eventually allowed a smile to break through that gruff exterior.

"I remember a time when a birthday party would have been the furthest thing from my brother's mind. He seems to be adjusting to single parenthood at last."

"The slide was a good idea," Sasha nodded. "The other kids will try to emulate it at their parties."

"Oh, I don't mean just that," Janice told her. "Jake's loosened up. I don't know how to explain it, exactly. He's more alive, more full of life than I've seen him for a long time." She cast a speculative glance over Sasha's tall form. "I think most of that is due to you."

Sasha shook her head. "I don't think I can take the credit for that. We don't even get along," she murmured softly, not wanting her voice to carry over the yard to the group still gathered around Cody.

"You were getting along quite well earlier," Janice observed, grinning at her. Her voice had a teasing quality that was reminiscent of Jake's in a good mood. Sasha shook her head.

"He might feel something for me," she told the older woman softly. "But even if he does, he won't acknowledge it. It's like he has a block where I'm concerned."

This time it was Janice who shook her head.

"Not you," she explained soberly. "Jake won't, or at least hasn't, allowed himself to feel that way about anyone since Angela. But I think you might be the one person who could draw him out from that shell he's erected. If you tried."

She motioned Sasha into a lawn chair and sank down

across from her, one eye peeled for any commotion at the other end of the lawn. Fortunately Jake seemed to have things well in hand.

"Angela was a wonderful woman, Sasha. She loved my brother and she was determined to be a good mother to their son. Unfortunately she was ill quite a lot. And sometimes she used it to make Jake feel guilty for not doing his share." Janice shook her head.

"Jake got his first church and they were fine for a while. But things got tough, communications within the congregation broke down and there was trouble. He figured it was somehow his fault. Of course it wasn't. But he needed somebody who would help him focus on the good things he'd done, the way he'd helped those people through some rough times. Angela couldn't do that."

"It would have been horrible for both of them," Sasha agreed.

"Angela loved that little boy," Janice murmured, watching Cody race across the lawn. "She felt responsible for raising him properly and she wanted Jake to share in those moments. But he was constantly tied up with meetings and she had to deal with Cody's colic and then teething on her own. She told me once that she felt Jake was dumping too much on her, that she had too much to cope with." Janice shrugged. "She probably did, but so did my brother."

"What happened?"

"Jake spent hours with the board, trying to ease the process. When they finally left that church, a rift had developed between Jake and his wife. Jake suggested that they take a family vacation to get away from everything. He loved her and he desperately wanted to show her that she and Cody were the most important people in his life, even though he hadn't been able to be there when she needed him. Unfortunately, she had an attack and died with Cody watching. Once more my brother felt guilty, as if he'd demanded too much of her."

"That explains it," Sasha murmured, thinking of his re-action to her "baby" plans.

"Pardon?" There were tears in the corners of Janice's big brown eyes.

Sasha shook her head. "Never mind," she said. This wasn't the time to explain her need to create her own family.

"He tried, Sasha. He tried really hard. But he was lost. His head office suggested he move to England to finish his studies. Then Cody began acting up."

Sasha sighed. "I don't suppose the nightmares helped Jake any."

Janice swiveled her head to stare. "You know?"

"I think it was one of the first things I learned," Sasha murmured sadly. She sat lost in her thoughts for a few moments before speaking once more. "I got the impression that Jake had never really discussed his wife's death with Cody in a way that the child could understand."

"Very astute." Janice grinned. "He's only been able to clear that up lately, he says. Partly because he left Cody's upbringing to our mother when they first flew over. The two of them became strangers." She heaved a sigh. "Thank goodness Mom finally put her foot down and went home."

"I feel badly for him, for them both," Sasha murmured. "But I still don't see what you think I can do to help, aside from being Cody's friend."

Janice studied her, wide serious eyes assessing in their scrutiny. "Jake's scared," she said at last. "Scared that he'll fail with Cody, scared that he'll blow this assignment, scared that he'll let someone get too close and then they'll see that he isn't this macho, in-control emissary of God who can handle all the problems of the world with his left thumb."

It wasn't a disparaging remark. Rather it reflected his sister's concern for her brother.

"What he needs is someone who will make him face up to the truth."

"Which is?" Sasha stared at his sister doubtfully.

Janice shrugged. "That love is an equal opportunity employer. You give some and the other person gives some and you both pull together."

"You're saying that marriage is a two-way street. Kind of a constant give and take. A mutual support group." Sasha peered at her new friend.

Janice nodded. "Yep, that's exactly what it is."

"What what is?" Jake stood behind them, a quizzical look on his face.

"Marriage," Janice told him promptly, without prevarication. "I was talking to Sasha about marriage."

"She doesn't want to know about marriage." Jake snorted. "She wants to know about child-rearing." He frowned, glaring at them both.

"That's not fair, Jake." Sasha got up as a yell of protest interrupted her. "I'll check it out," she murmured, moving away to regain her perspective on the situation. "You two relax."

"What did you say to her?" he demanded, surveying his sister's smug look.

"Oh, just a little girl talk."

He searched her blank face for a clue.

"I hate it when you do that," he growled. "Are you sure you weren't trying your hand at matchmaking? Especially after what you saw in the kitchen?" He had to admit, Janice's face was blank with astonishment.

"You know that's never been my style," she reminded him cheerfully. "I've always gone for the direct approach."

"I know." He grimaced. "I don't want you meddling, Jan. Regardless of what you think, I don't want to get married again. I can't." Jake felt stupid saying it, but he had to make sure she understood.

Janice smiled brightly. "Sure you can. And you will."

As she met his angry look, Janice fluttered her hands in the air. "But I'm sure you will handle it in your own good time, brother dear. Meanwhile Sasha and I were just getting acquainted. I like her."

She made it sound like a benediction. Jake fumed. As if his sister had given *Good Housekeeping*'s Seal of Approval on their friendship. Or acquaintance. Or whatever it was!

"Did she tell you about her baby?"

Janice's eyebrows rose in amazement. "She's pregnant?"

Jake shook his head and called himself a fool for sticking a foot into it again. "No! Never mind. She'll tell you when she's ready."

Janice rose from her chair with the lithe grace of a cobra ready for the kill. Her fingernails dangled toward him, red and long and lethal.

"Oh, no, you don't. Not to me. What about this baby?"

Grimly Jake gave her the details. It bugged him to even say the words "artificial insemination" let alone about someone like Sasha. Especially to his sister! The least Janice could have done was back up his opinion.

"I think it's fantastic. That someone should want a child so badly that they would let themselves go through that awful clinical procedure means that it's very important to them." Janice grinned at him. "She'll be a fantastic mother. Look at her."

Jake looked. He had to admit the calm casual approach Sasha used to deal with each youngster without so much as a raised voice or a hair out of place was impressive. Without reservation, the children obeyed her strictures to wash their grubby paws after playing in the bubble solution and then laughed merrily as they ganged up to blow a barrage of bubbles in her face.

The wanton he'd caught a glimpse of in the kitchen was gone now, supplanted by a Venus in hip-hugging, ice-cream-splattered white shorts and a purple tank top that gaped a little in the front. Her skin glowed with a light tan that gave her complexion a luminosity most women envied. But she didn't have an ounce of makeup on and her black cap of hair was mussed, he noted absently. She had a softness about her that Jake found very appealing and he damped it down with anger.

"She's lovely, isn't she?" Janice murmured behind him.

Jake turned and caught the calculating look on her face. "She's not my type," he commented in a flat voice. He wheeled away to pick up the paper and ribbons littering his lawn. "Not my type at all."

Janice peered at him through narrowed eyes.

"*Au contraire,* my dear brother. She is exactly your type—strong and loyal and dependable. But I wonder how long it will take you to see it for yourself?"

Chapter Eight

"I'm sorry, dear, I really hate to ask but I simply cannot go in today. I feel wretched." Flora Brown's weak, wispy voice barely carried over the phone line.

Sasha groaned inwardly, setting aside the store accounts she had taken the day off to work on. Deidre plopped a mug of coffee in front of her before moving back into the store to answer the bell's urgent summons.

"But, Flora, I've got a pile of work to do. What about Janice Windsor? Couldn't she help?"

Flora's voice sounded slightly stronger.

"If you'd been in church last week," she chided, "you would have known that Janice *Armstrong*—" definite emphasis on the last name "—and her daughter had to leave. Her husband needed her."

Sasha accepted the rebuke. Flora couldn't be expected to know that she had deliberately avoided attending the services last week expressly to evade the pastor and his family.

"What has to be done?" she asked the older woman at last. No one would have termed it gracefully.

When Sasha went into the small church office an hour

later, she was mentally kicking and screaming all the way. What she really needed, she told herself, was distance to try to sort out the crazy emotions she had experienced in Jake's arms. What she didn't need was further contact with him and more complications in her hitherto ordinary life.

The information for the bulletins was placed neatly in the file folder Flora had mentioned and Sasha immediately began inputting the data onto the church computer, implementing the standard format Flora had used for years.

The usual notices about the ladies' meetings and choir practice were there as well as one announcing a baby shower. She was deep into a *Clip Art* book, searching for the appropriate caricatures when the door opened and Jake Windsor sauntered in.

Sasha forced herself to glance up calmly and then took a second surprised look. He looked ghastly.

"Morning," he mumbled, edging past her to his tiny office.

"Good morning." Privately Sasha wondered how long he'd been awake. His beard was at least one day old and his hair drooped over his eyebrow as if he hadn't combed it for days. He wore a white shirt and black slacks but they looked as if he'd slept in them and there was certainly no evidence of his usual zest for life.

She moved silently to the door of his office and saw him rake his hands through his untidy hair. It was a gesture of tiredness combined with frustration.

"Would you like a cup of coffee?" she asked softly, unwilling to venture too far into the lion's den.

"Lord, no." It was definite, she'd give him that. She shrugged and moved to leave. "I don't think my stomach would tolerate it," he told her sullenly.

"You're ill," she exclaimed, noting the pasty-white condition of his skin.

"Oh, really? I hadn't noticed." He glared at her balefully. "Is the bulletin ready for a proof yet?"

Sasha nodded.

"Just doing the artwork. Flora's ill, too. She phoned me to fill in." As he opened his mouth to protest, Sasha held up her hand. "It's all right. I've done it before. But I'll get a copy for you to glance over." She scurried out the door and then peeked her head back in as he mumbled something. "Pardon?"

"I said, I'm sure the bulletin's fine. I just wondered if Miss Brown was okay." Jake rubbed the back of his neck wearily. His face was a shade greener now.

"She's fine. Flu, I think. I stopped in just before I came here. She's resting this morning. Apparently everyone's getting sick. Must be a bug."

He made a few suggestions on changes he wanted made before he lurched to his feet and stumbled over to the bookshelf. When he returned with a huge black tome, Sasha noticed his hand shaking. He sank into his chair with obvious relief, whitened fingers grasping the edge of the desk.

"Go home," she ordered. "I'll finish everything here. You go and relax." She sauntered to the door before she remembered. "Where's Cody?"

He had his head in his hands and when he finally tilted it to look up at her, his eyes were bleary and bloodshot. His voice was hoarse and it was clearly an effort to speak.

"Gone to the city with a busload of kids. Children's Festival."

She nodded. "Yes, I remember."

He hauled himself to his feet unsteadily as she watched, standing teetering for a few moments before starting toward the door with slow halting movements. As she observed his actions, he suddenly reached out and grabbed the back of a chair, eyes closing.

His craggily handsome face was wet with perspiration. Droplets ran down his forehead and tangled in those long black lashes and Sasha could see spots of feverish pink high on his cheekbones.

"What in the world are you trying to do, spread your germs around?" She berated him, wrapping one arm around his waist and offering her shoulder for him to lean against.

"Come on. You're going home. To bed. Mrs. Garner can make you some soup or something."

He leaned against her heavily. His strength had obviously almost gone.

"She can't," he muttered in a gasp. "She's sick, too."

"Oh, for heaven's sake." It wasn't appropriate to light into him then and there, while he was sucking in deep lungsful of air. Not fair to castigate him for his stupid male pride when Jake Windsor could barely totter down the few steps to her car, never mind walk up the driveway of his home not fifty yards away.

But later, Sasha vowed to herself. She'd let him have it later on when he was better able to hear and understand exactly what she had to say about bullheaded men who didn't know when to give in.

As she led him inside and helped him up the stairs, Sasha felt her own forehead perspire with the effort of supporting his not inconsiderable weight. Jake was weak now, barely able to negotiate the area from the doorway to his bed. He flopped onto it with a groan and rested his head gingerly on the cool cotton surface of his pillow.

"I beg your pardon," she asked when his low voice rumbled something.

"I feel like crap," he muttered.

Sasha grinned, untying and tugging off his shoes. "You don't look much better," she teased. "How many sour balls did you eat?"

He groaned and propped one eye open to stare at her balefully.

"Not funny," he grunted, pushing under the blankets and tugging them up to his ears. His long, lean body shivered beneath them. "Can't get warm," he said through chattering teeth.

Sasha lifted the thick handmade quilt from the stand across his room and laid it over him.

"This should help. It's a lovely piece of handwork." She stared down at the tiny even stitches that covered the wedding ring pattern. It had been carefully sewn together, the colors ranging from softest pink to deep luscious rose. Jake whispered something.

"What did you say?" she asked, brushing the black lock of hair off his bronzed forehead. He looked like a gigantic Cody, cuddled into the bed like that.

Sasha leaned closer. But his eyes, when he batted them open, were shiny with fever and blazed at her with glittering silver sparks.

"Angela made that," he whispered hoarsely. "She doesn't like to use it." A second later his beautiful gray eyes closed and he sank back into his pillows, snoring softly.

Sasha shook her head. It was a strange attitude, but one she'd seen often enough in her store. Some women purchased beautiful articles for their home and then stored them carefully away to be occasionally taken out and admired. She would prefer to use the quilt and enjoy its beauty every day, if this were her home.

She moved down the stairs to the kitchen and met a white-faced, shaky Mrs. Garner refilling a small pitcher in the kitchen.

"You, too." She smiled empathetically.

"It's very draining." The older woman nodded slowly. "I feel as weak as a kitten. I thought if I could have a cup of tea or something, perhaps..." Her murmuring voice died away.

"I'll get this for you. You go climb into bed. I was just going to make a warm drink for Pastor Jake. He's got it, too." Sasha took the container out of her hand.

"Oh, dear. How can we deal with young Cody, now?" A frown creased Mrs. Garner's delicate porcelain skin as her hands fluttered uselessly by her sides. She pressed away from the counter tiredly.

"I'll bring him home when the bus comes back. You're not to worry. Just rest and get well." Carefully, slowly, she helped the older woman back to her room.

By the time the kettle boiled and she had taken the tea in to Mrs. Garner, the housekeeper was sleeping, a noisy gurgle emanating from the depths of her open mouth.

Then, succumbing to the inevitable, Sasha climbed the stairs to Jake's room. She wouldn't leave a sick cat, Sasha muttered to her laughing subconscious. She could hardly leave the gray-faced, weakly minister to fend for himself at a time like this.

He was awake, but it was a feverish awakeness that sent a warning through Sasha. He still had the high bright spots of color and his face was dripping with sweat. He'd removed his clothes, she noticed, picking up the discarded objects from a pile on the middle of the floor.

"What are you doing here?" It was a gruff demand that came out in a croaky voice.

"I took Mrs. Garner a drink of tea. She's ill, too." Sasha set down the drink she'd made for him on the nightstand and felt his forehead.

"It's just a bug. I'll be fine in a little while." He glared up at her, struggling to find a more comfortable position in the wide bed. Sasha heard him groan as his arms refused to support him for more than a few seconds.

Privately, she grinned. A little while was going to be about a week long, if she figured accurately. But she knew better than to say it. Instead she held the mug out toward him.

"Drink this. You are probably dehydrated and need to take in fluids."

"I'm fine," he mumbled, but his fingers fumbled as they

closed around the china, grazing hers. Sasha hung on, noticing the increasing weakness in his shaking hand. "What is this?"

"Just something to help you feel better. And maybe sleep."

"Oh." He sipped a bit and then lay his head back down. "I feel so weak," he complained. "I was fine last night. I even mowed the church lawn."

Sasha kept her mouth shut, merely pressing her hand behind his shoulders to offer another sip from the steaming cup. In fact, Jake took several before turning his head away and flopping back onto the pillows.

"No more. I feel very strange." His eyes were very bright, the pupils huge in his flushed face.

She sat there on the edge of the bed for a few moments longer until the ludicrously long lashes flopped against his lean cheek.

"Go to sleep," she murmured. "When you wake up it will probably flush right out of your system."

She lifted one hand reluctantly and smoothed the burnished lock of sweat-moistened hair off his brow. As she laid her palm against his heated skin, Sasha frowned. He seemed warmer now than before. She wondered how much aspirin he'd already consumed, whether it was safe to offer more.

The mug was within his reach on the dresser when she began to get up. She didn't notice any change in his demeanor until, like a whip, his hand reached out from under the blankets and fastened around her wrist. Her eyes flew to Jake's face. They were wide open and glittering with a strange light.

"I'll have another drink of that stuff you've concocted," he rasped, watching her bring the cup toward him. "You don't have to help me," he grunted. "I can sit up by myself."

He pressed against the mattress, but eventually gave up as his head flopped back onto the pillows with a groan.

"Or not," she heard him mutter.

Once more, Sasha slid her arm behind his shoulders and supported him while he took a long, thirsty drink, draining the pottery mug.

"You should go easy on that," she advised, staring into his face as she tried to assess the fever. "I put a little bit of alcohol in it to soothe your throat. I hope you don't mind."

At least she thought it was a little. She wasn't a drinker but half and half—half whiskey, half tea—seemed about right. At least he was relaxing now with his eyes closed. She sat watching him, memorizing each dear feature. A lazy smile flickered across his handsome face as she tried unsuccessfully to remove her arm.

"I don't mind," he breathed happily. "I don't mind at all." Jake pressed further back into the mattress, trapping her arm behind him and tugging her forward with his other hand.

Where had this sudden strength come from? she wondered curiously, trying to free herself unobtrusively. A moment ago he hadn't been able to hold his head to the cup, now he was pinning her against the side of the bed with one muscular, *bare* leg.

"Um, excuse me? Pastor Windsor? Jake?"

His big gray eyes flopped open again as he smiled a silly grin at her.

"You can call me Jake," he whispered. "I like it when you do that." His hand tightened on her arm, tugging her down toward his face. "A kiss always makes everything all better," he drawled, his gray eyes glittering strangely. "Kiss me!"

There were probably several alternatives she could have taken, but Sasha didn't consider anything but complying with his request. He was sick, after all. And in a delirium by the feel of his fingers around her wrist. He probably thought she was someone else. And anyway, she wanted to kiss those soft lips. Just once more.

Carefully she leaned forward and then, changing her mind, brushed her mouth across his cheek. That was more motherly, not so provocative. "There. Now go to sleep. Try to rest."

"I'd like to sleep. With you. But I wouldn't kiss you like that." He grinned that stupid vacant smile that twigged some hidden memory in Sasha's mind. What in the world was wrong with him?

Suddenly his hand jerked her forward and she fell splayed across his bare chest, her fingers tingling as they slipped across the bronzed sheen of his chest. The only thing between their bodies were the covers, which were now dragged down to his waist.

"Jake, I think you…" Her voice trailed away as his hand moved slowly up and down her back in a soft, tantalizing caress.

"I like how you feel," he muttered. "Cool and comfortable. Like a woman. I like a woman who is strong and capable."

Sasha felt the flush of red stain her cheeks. He was a minister, for heaven's sake. She shouldn't be hearing this. He shouldn't be saying it to her, even if she wanted to hear it.

His face buried itself into the curve of her shoulder, nudging the fabric aside. "Smells like flowers. I like flowers."

He's just delirious, she told herself. He thinks you're someone else. He'll snap out of it pretty soon.

Sasha tried to get her head up to assess the look on his face. His hand was tangled in her hair, but he let her move slightly away. His eyes were open, staring at her hotly as he wrapped his other arm around her back.

"I've wanted to do this for so long," he muttered, brushing his hand across her back, tracing the line of her backbone. Seconds later the teeth on her zipper parted and she gasped as his hot hands slipped under the fabric of her dress to slide across her back.

"Soft, so soft." His mouth nuzzled her neck, touching her skin in little nips.

Sasha choked as she felt his fingers slide to the clasp of her bra. She had to get out of here. Now!

"Jake, don't. I have to go." His mouth was hovering near hers as she struggled against him. "I have to go back to the church," she muttered, hoping he'd snap out of it.

Instead he pulled her more fully onto the bed, on top of him. She could feel the hard, pulsing length of him through the thin covers and her cotton dress. Unfortunately, Angela's quilt had long since slipped to the floor.

"Don't go." His lips whispered it into the shell of her ear. "It's been so long—so long since anybody cared. You care about me, don't you?"

Sasha shook with desire and nerves and frustration all at the same time. "Jake, I don't think…"

"No," he muttered. "Don't think. Don't think at all. Just kiss me. I like it when you do that. I like kissing you. You give yourself…" The words were slurred as his head fell forward, against her.

Suddenly it all fell together. Drunk! He was drunk on the combination of fever and alcohol. No different than Dwain. Oh, Lord! What had she been thinking to get the minister of First Avenue soused?

"Aren't you going to kiss me?" he asked drowsily, his eyelids flopping closed on those big gray eyes. "I like kissing…"

Even smashed, he's adorable. She shrugged the thought away. Gently her hand smoothed the black hair away from his face. No one could see. No one would know.

Giving in to the impulse, Sasha softly pressed her lips to his, pouring all her love into the tender caress and letting his smooth, soft lips kiss her back. It felt so right, so wonderful. And it would never end.

"Are you and my dad getting married now?"

With a gasp of dismay, Sasha jerked herself out of Jake's slack embrace and turned toward the door. Cody and Bobby stood together staring at the picture of Sasha spread across the bed, draped across the Reverend Jacob Windsor's seminude body, with her dress undone.

And standing behind the two children was none other than Horace Mealey: bus driver for the children's excursion and chairman of the board of First Avenue Church.

Chapter Nine

"Well, we can't play in my yard. There's a 'portant meeting goin' on at the church and my dad don't want no noise."

Sasha moved a little nearer to the open doorway. Church meeting? Why hadn't she been informed?

"I know. My dad's goin', too." Bobby's voice was full of smug superiority. "He said he's going to find out just what kind of minister we got. Your dad's in big trouble now, Cody."

Oh, no! The words penetrated her brain as a tide of red covered her cheeks. Horace had obviously organized some kind of a congregational get-together after witnessing that little scene at the manse last week. She had tried desperately to explain the situation to him. Obviously without success. Sasha could just imagine all the curious little busybodies that would show up to hear the gossip.

"God answered my prayers." That was Cody, trying to one-up his pal. Sasha smiled as she eavesdropped. "I'm gettin' a new mom, ya know." The smile left her face. Jake was getting married?

"Nah, you're not. Sasha ain't marryin' your dad. You're gonna be moving away and she's gotta stay here to run her store." There was a grunt and then Cody started crying.

"Are not! I'm not moving. Not ever."

Bobby's jeers grew louder and nastier until Cody was shrieking with anger. "You're lying," he bellowed.

Gritting her teeth, Sasha stepped out onto the street and separated the two. "Go home, Bobby. And no more fighting. I'm going to be speaking to your mom about this."

She nudged Cody inside Bednob's and put the Back in Five Minutes sign on the door. He was sobbing his little heart out and it took some time to calm him down. Finally, with his bony body snuggled up to hers, she asked the question.

"Cody, why do you think your dad and I are getting married?" His brown eyes stared up at her.

"Cause I saw you on the bed together. That's what mommies and daddies do. I tol' them all about that, but they wouldn't listen."

She groaned inwardly. He'd broadcasted her indiscretions all over town, it seemed. Her self-castigation ended as she caught sight of his tear-stained little face.

"I want you for my mom, Sasha. I prayed and prayed about it for a long time." He sniffed pathetically. "My dad needs you, too."

"Oh, Cody. I would love to be your mommy. I think you're the greatest little boy I've ever known. You're very special to me." She brushed the soft brown hair back and hugged him close.

"Then how come don't you and my dad get married? We could be a family." He peered up at her with those big brown, heart-searching eyes.

Sasha swallowed. She wanted to hold him tight, cuddle his little body near her heart and protect him from all the hurts. He wasn't just any child, he was Jake's son. And she wanted to share the privilege of parenting Cody with him.

But it wasn't going to happen. Not now. Not ever. And there was no way she was going to lie to him about the possibility.

"Cody, your dad doesn't want to marry me. He doesn't love me. You see that's what grown-ups need to get married and be happy together."

"But you love him and me, doncha?" Cody squinted up at her. "Couldn't you just love us 'nough to go around? I've got lots of love an' I could share." He wrapped his sturdy little arms around her neck and hugged her tightly against him.

Sasha wiped away the tear that formed at his words. He was so dear, so precious. How could she not love him? How could she let him go? Carefully, gently, she set the little boy down beside her.

"Listen to me, sweetie." He turned his tear-stained face up trustingly. "Sometimes things don't go exactly the way we want, Cody. You love me and I love you and that's great. We can do that." She tweaked his nose. "And that's not ever gonna change. Not ever. Okay?"

He nodded.

"I love your dad, too, but I can't make your dad love me. He has to decide things like that for himself. And he has. He doesn't want to get married again. Do you understand?"

Cody's dark head shook. "No! I prayed and prayed and Dad said God always answers our prayers." His bottom lip jutted out stubbornly.

Sasha smiled. He looked so much like his father, her heart ached with sadness for what would never be.

"Cody?"

"What?" He glared at her.

"Sometimes God says no."

He jumped up, tugging himself out of her embrace. His dark eyes flashed with anger. "No, he doesn't. Just adults do. 'No, you can't have a mom. No, you can't have a brother. No, you can't be like other kids.'" He raced to the door and yanked it open. His brown eyes flashed with fury as he glared back at her.

"I hate you. I hate all of you!"

Sasha got to her feet with a sigh. You didn't handle that well, she told herself. Not well at all.

Perhaps you should consider taking a few mothering lessons before you embark on your next project, Sasha.

"Oh, shut up, would you?" She spit the words out to stop that nagging little voice inside her head. The door chime rang in response to her bid for peace.

"Hey, girl. What're you doing back here?" Deidre's curious face peered down at her, her voice questioning. "Are you okay?"

Meeting her friend's inquisitive glance made Sasha smile. If only she knew!

"The question is, what're you doing here, Didi? No good-looking guys available on a Thursday evening?"

Didi stuck out her tongue. "Just came to see if you'd heard the latest about our new Rev. Big meeting going on. I hear some are trying to fire him."

"What! Fire him for what—getting sick?"

"What's the matter with you, Sash? Anyone would think you were personally involved." Deidre stared at her.

Sasha stared right back at her, a tide of red suffusing her mind. Jake was in this mess because of her. And even though he wasn't totally innocent, she wasn't going to sit back and let him take the rap for something that was both their faults. Sasha Lambert was no weak-kneed, lily-livered wimp.

"I am personally involved," she murmured, sucking in a deep breath for courage and straightening her shoulders. She checked the store quickly before glancing back at Deidre. "Have you got an hour or so to spare, pal? I need your help."

* * *

"Miss Lambert, this is a private meeting. The public is not permitted to speak."

Jake watched in fascination as Sasha glared at the sanctimonious curmudgeon who had ruled First Avenue Church for more than a decade. Horace, it seemed, had met his match.

"I intend to speak at this meeting, Horace, and I don't care whether you like it or not. If you don't let me have my say here, I'll do it on the front lawn and the whole town will really have something to talk about."

She leaned toward the old man and whispered something in his ear. That florid face blanched, Jake noted, watching Horace step back as if he'd been bitten.

Sasha marched past him and glanced around the sanctuary, noting each participant. Her eyes lingered on him for several moments before she turned away. He thought he glimpsed pain in those expressive green eyes. But then, Sasha had never been good at hiding her emotions.

"Ladies and gentlemen. I want to clarify something for all of you here today. Despite what you may have heard, nothing—*absolutely nothing* untoward occurred between myself and Jacob Windsor."

He sat up straight.

"Now wait just a minute here. I don't need anybody—"

She cut him off, chest heaving. "Shut up, Jake. I'm speaking. You can have your say when I'm finished. And please control your tongue."

"Yes, Reverend. I think we'd all like to know what strange event occurred that propelled Miss Lambert into your bedroom, on your bed, with her dress unzipped."

Jake stared across the table at Hector Bratley. His eyes narrowed at the look of smug self-righteousness covering the man's fleshy face but Sasha rushed in to speech before he could punch the guy's lights out.

"That would all be very nice, Hector, if we thought you didn't have just a tinge of dirt under your own nails. Where do you go every Sunday morning, anyway?'' Sasha's quelling tones were loud and defiant. Jake grinned at the flush of red that covered the man's cheeks. "Some people *say* that you're fishing," she hinted. "I've always wondered."

Jake leaned back with a beam of admiration tickling the edges of his mouth. Sasha Lambert was no shrinking wallflower. She sure as heck didn't need him to help her. He'd let her have her say. She could handle them. All of them. For now.

"I don't really think this is appropriate, Miss Lambert." That was Sydney Lowell, Jake noted, and nodded to himself. It figured. The undertaker was always concerned with the proprieties. "This is an unofficial gathering that—''

"That's usually the way dirty business is conducted, isn't it, Syd? Those sneaky little lies and innuendos that ruin reputations never get to see the light of day. Well, I'm not being a party to it. You've got the best minister we've had in years and you're trying to ruin him."

Jake noted the way her generous chest heaved in indignation. He shifted uncomfortably as he remembered the press of those abundant curves against his body. He watched her eyes slice through the heavy atmosphere, homing in on each of them.

"But, Miss Lambert, you were seen in the reverend's own *bedroom,* for gracious' sake."

"And you're going to blacken my name, too, John Simkins? Without even asking for more information?'' She laughed shortly.

"I saw the reverend leaving her house very early one morning," Ingolf Handers added self-righteously. "It was just after Mrs. Tate passed on." His beady black eyes riveted on Jake's red face.

"Gentlemen, gentlemen," Sasha scolded, wagging one finger. "Aren't I a member of this congregation? Couldn't I have requested the minister's assistance with a small problem at my business?"

Jake could see the curiosity eating away at the elderly men. Well, let them wonder! He was sure Sasha wasn't going to bring fine, upstanding *drunk* Dwain into this conversation on morals. His admiration for her made his chest swell with pride. She had more courage than the whole lot!

"Now listen well, for I'm going to tell you the facts, gentlemen. And I defy you to make anything of them." She glared at them angrily as she told the tale.

"The truth is that I was asked to fill in for Flora. She was ill. So was Pastor Jake. So was Mrs. Garner. I noted this fact and tried to help out. Did my Christian duty, if you will. I thought it was appropriate to bring the pastor's high fever down with a liberal dose of alcohol in the tea I made. I am not as familiar with the substance as some of you," she noted, glaring at Hector once more. "I must have used too much."

Her cheeks suffused in a most becoming pink. Jake stared at her curiously, wondering at the blossoming color that was getting darker by the moment. He didn't remember any alcohol. Just a warm fuzziness that had eased through his aching muscles.

"Either that, or Reverend Windsor was delirious."

Jake was tempted to laugh. Not so delirious that the pastor in question couldn't remember the feel of her long, lithe body against his, he wanted to tell her. Or the way her mouth molded to his. Or the way those soft gentle hands had touched him. And he sure as heck remembered the way she'd kissed him. He felt his cheeks heat. Boy, did he remember!

"In any case, the pastor mistakenly thought I was his wife. No doubt he misses Mrs. Windsor still and in his disturbed state of mind, believed I was she." Sasha's voice was soft and full of...pain?

His mouth was hanging open. Jake could feel it. But he was powerless to close it. He wasn't sure which he resented more—Sasha saying he didn't know whom he'd held in his arms or intimating that he was mentally unstable. But Sasha barreled along, intent on clearing his reputation while quite possibly ruining her own.

"I only know that he lapsed into unconsciousness and I was trying to extricate myself from that situation when Cody and everyone arrived."

She fixed them all with that piercing gaze that dared anyone to refute her words.

"Ladies and gentlemen, if you disseminate this mendacious lie you have concocted throughout the community, I shall have no recourse but to acquire a legal opinion on the slander I have suffered. This disinformation is defamatory in the extreme and totally without foundation. I insist you put an end to this ridiculous meeting. Good day."

Jake watched her storm out of the room with a spark of mirth begging to be released. Her head was high in the air, her back ramrod straight. He could even see the sparks shimmer off her shiny black hair. She must have searched long and hard for those bits of linguistic nonsense she had tossed out so indiscriminately, he decided.

He smiled. It felt good to have someone to stand up for him, even if he preferred to fight his own battles. It was something Angela would never have been strong enough to do—something he would have never asked her to do. Yet it felt wonderful. As if Sasha really cared for him and was willing to take on the miscreants in the congregation to prove it.

Of course, he told himself briskly, it was totally unnecessary. These people had no business questioning his morals. They should know by now that he had no intention of forming any personal relationships. Not of that type.

The group sat silent, staring at each other in confusion.

"I didn't understand anything she said after that bit about the reverend getting delirious and all mixed up," Marv Seevers muttered. "Danged highfalutin language. What's wrong with the woman's English?"

Jake glanced at Horace. The old coot looked like he was going to faint. It was time to assume control, Jake decided. Way past time to take charge of his own life. He had Sasha to thank for that at least. He knew he wasn't going to stand quietly by any longer, no matter what they decided. He stood and faced them all calmly.

"Folks, I am going to leave you now. I believe the rest of this meeting should be conducted without me. I can only assure you once more that I am extremely sorry for any of my actions that might have been misconstrued by you. Good day."

With voices hissing and whispering behind him, Jake straightened his shoulders and sauntered calmly out of the church and across the lawn. As he walked he chastised himself for his stupidity. Of all the irresponsible, unacceptable things for a minister to do, coming on to a parishioner, particularly one as lovely as Sasha Lambert.

Not that he was sorry. He'd wasted hours wondering how her lips would feel. His only regret about the whole incident was that they'd been caught in such a compromising position. It was another black mark against his career and on Sasha's reputation. But mostly, he regretted that he'd been too muzzy to fully appreciate the effect she'd had on him. That was some lady!

He was still thinking about it when Mrs. Garner stopped him at the door of his study. "Reverend, I think you need to speak to Cody. He's been very upset. I can't seem to find out the problem."

Jake sighed. Just what he needed. Another confrontation with Cody. The boy was obsessed with this family thing. And totally infatuated with Sasha Lambert.

So why wouldn't he be? His own father couldn't stop thinking about her! Jake ignored the mocking little voice inside his head.

"Thanks, Esther. I'll go now. Would you mind putting

on a pot of coffee? I have a feeling it's going to be a long night.''

He walked down the hallway slowly, trying to summon strength as he rapped lightly on the closed door.

"Cody? What's wrong, son?"

His six-year-old son sat on his bed surrounded by chaos. Toys, clothes, games and books littered the room. Jake felt an unassailable panic tighten around his lungs. Right then he could have used a shoulder to hang on to and just this once he could have used some good, sensible advice from somebody stronger than he. Somebody capable and solid. Someone like Sasha.

He shook the thought away angrily. He'd pushed her away. There was no one else to be had. There was just himself and Cody in this family. That was the way he wanted it.

Wasn't it?

"Cody?"

"I'm not talking to you." Jake could hear shades of Bobby Bratley's defiance in his tones and grimaced. Regardless of what Sasha said, that kid was bratty.

"Mind your manners, Cody. I'm still your father. Now calm down and tell me what seems to be the problem." He tried to tug the little form onto his lap but Cody resisted.

"Sasha says there is so a God, but I don't believe her." He uttered it in a quick little rush that dared Jake to contradict him. His round little face, when he tipped it up, was full of dirty tear stains. He gulped down a sob.

"Why?" Jake tried to stifle the panic he felt. How do I handle this new challenge? he appealed silently.

"'Cause I prayed hard as I knowed how for a mom. I been good. I didn't tear my jeans no more. An' I leaved Goldie in her bowl so she wouldn't get dead like Henry." His voice was full of self-righteous indignation. "An' Sasha says that stuff don't matter cause she can't be my mom no way.'' He brushed his grimy fist across his face and glared up at his dad. ''An' you know why?''

Jake shook his head helplessly. He didn't want to go down this route but it seemed there was no way out.

''Sasha says she loves me real bad. An' she tol' me she loves you, too. But she can't be my mom 'cause she hasn't got 'nough love to make you have some, too. If you won't love her by your own self, she doesn't want to be in our family.'' Cody's tanned face glared defiantly up at his father. ''Well then, I don't want to be in it, neither. Not unless you get some love in your heart.''

Jake felt drained, totally devoid of any emotion. Sasha loved him. He knew it as clearly as if she'd said it out loud.

But he wouldn't love her back. He couldn't open himself up to all that pain and disappointment again. He'd get over needing to feel those long slim arms around him and so would Cody. They had to didn't they? She wouldn't want to be tied to someone like him—someone who spoiled everything.

''Cody, I know you like Sasha. And Bobby. And lots of other things about Allen's Springs. And we have had a good time here. But we might have to move on soon. You'll meet new friends, even start in a new school in the fall.'' Jake looked down in surprise as his son cried out.

''Nn-noo-oo!'' It was a wail that pierced Jake's heart. ''You can't. You can't.'' The boy sobbed the words over and over again, flailing his skinny arms out at his father.

''I know it's hard, Cody. But Auntie Janice and Cousin Kate will come visit us in our new place. You'll like it. So will I. Really.'' It was the first time Jake could ever remember deliberately lying to his son.

Cody pulled away, hunched over and sniffling at the other end of the bed. He said nothing for a long time. Finally his glossy brown head lifted and he stared at his father sadly, round eyes welling with tears.

"Don't you even like her a little bit?" he asked softly, hiccuping with sobs.

Jake stared at the needlepoint picture Angela had made before Cody's birth. But it wasn't his wife's face he saw there. It was a pair of laughing jade eyes peering out from beneath short spiky black hair. It was that infectious chuckle that he heard and those long, long legs he saw.

He brushed it all away with one blink of an eye.

"Yes, son. I like her a lot. But I'm not going to marry her." Having just dashed his son's hopes, Jake moved disconsolately toward the door. "It's been a tough day, Cody. I want you to clean up this mess and then get ready for bed. I'll come and tuck you up in twenty minutes."

Cody was staring at him, head cocked to one side.

"Cody?" He searched for some clue in those unfathomable brown eyes.

His son twisted away from his scrutiny, scooping up his teddy in one hand and a pile of Lego blocks in the other.

"It's okay, Dad," he muttered. "I can get myself to bed. I don't need to be tucked in." Cody held the doorknob with one small fist. "Good night, Dad," he said, lower lip wobbling.

Jake smiled lopsidedly. The kid was telling him to get out. He was a strong boy, tough and resilient. He would handle this latest crisis. They both would. He ruffled the dark shining head.

"Good night, son. I love you."

The door closed softly behind him as Jake listened for the softly murmured reply. For the first time since Cody had begun to speak, there was no "Night, Dad" from the little tyke.

Jake sauntered down the hall to the kitchen and filled the biggest mug in the cupboard with strong black coffee.

"Somebody should tell her that single parenthood is harder than even I thought," he muttered, going through the door to the study to search the literature for any open postings somewhere far away from Allen's Springs.

He had to do it now. Before he could change his mind.

The knocking at the front door startled Jake out of his reverie. He lifted his feet off the desk, noticing the sheaf of Help Wanted papers that fell to the floor as he did. There were several possibilities in that stack. And all of them reminded him of Sasha, standing in his kitchen, begging him to own up to his own feelings.

"Yes?" Horace stood on the step with several other men behind him. They wore abashed expressions on their faces. "Would you like to come in?" He held the door wide and they trooped through to stand discomfited in his front hall.

"I... I mean, we... The thing is, Pastor, we made a mistake." Marv Seevers was muttering the words but the others all nodded their agreement. "After you left we got to discussing things and then some of the ladies came and..." His voice died away in embarrassment.

"What Marv means—" John Simkins took over, face red and sweating "—is that we had no business questioning you. Miss Lambert was right. You've been a danged good—I mean, real good minister to us and we know you wouldn't go against your principles like that. We'd like to apologize for tonight and ask you to stay on as our pastor." He grinned and thrust out one hand. "Fact is, we'd like to have you and Cody with us a good long time."

Jake stood gaping at them, his bare feet curling on the tiles as he took in their grinning faces and outstretched hands.

"Well, yes. Of course. I mean, yes, we'd like to stay." He shook hands until his arm felt as if it would fall off.

Ingolf Handers clapped him on the back with a smile as wide as the sky. "Fact is, Reverend—" he winked merrily "—Sasha Lambert would make a real good minister's wife. She's got guts, that lady. And determination. Nothing cows that girl. She sticks by what she believes.'' Ingolf chuckled. ''I guess she believes in you pretty strongly, Reverend.''

With their good wishes and boisterous apologies ringing in his ears, Jake sat on his front step under the stars and considered what he'd just heard.

It was true, all of it. Sasha Lambert was no shrinking violet. In fact, in that respect she was as far from Angela as a woman could get. She had stood up in front of his congregation and her friends with determination, unencumbered by her own fears and without any possible personal benefit. She hadn't been afraid of what they thought and she sure wasn't angling for a father for her child just then. No, she'd honestly tried to help him. Sasha had gone to such lengths simply because she thought it was her duty.

Jake grinned. She'd stood there, straight and tall, and as much as told him he was a wimp. It was true. He had wimped out on life because he wasn't willing to recognize or trust the lengths she was willing to go to, to save his good name, to help him keep his church, to support him.

And Lord knew, it couldn't have been easy. First of all, she had kissed him like a woman kisses the man she loves and he darned sure wasn't confused about that, alcohol or not! She had cared for him and nursed him, gone the extra mile and he'd let her! Leaned on a woman and accepted her strength. And enjoyed it!

''With Angela you always felt you had to be the strong one, brother dear,'' Janice had chided him. ''But Sasha's the kind of woman who pulls her own weight in a relationship. She wouldn't demand any more than you could give and she'd be ready to support you when you needed a hand up. That's real love.''

He stared at the houses lined along the avenue and whispered a prayer for direction. Although his life wasn't spinning wildly anymore, he still didn't feel in control. He still felt vulnerable and exposed. Defenseless. Could he afford to let anyone into his life again?

No, Jake, the small voice inside his heart whispered. *The question is, can you afford to leave Sasha Lambert out?*

And deep inside, he wondered if he had the courage to answer that.

Chapter Ten

Sasha picked up the brown kraft envelope and tucked it inside her purse before glancing around the room once more.

D-day. At last.

Any maudlin sentimentality for what might have been would not be tolerated. She was moving into a new phase of her life. So be it.

She had just locked the door when she felt the hand on her arm. It was Jake.

Not this morning, she prayed, bargaining with everything she could think of. *Not now!*

But when she opened her eyes, he was still there. Tall, handsome. Disheveled?

"What's the matter?" she demanded warily.

"Have you seen Cody this morning?" His frantic gray eyes searched hers.

Sasha frowned. He sounded odd, distraught even. "Cody? No. Why?"

He held out a small ragged section of what looked like

the church bulletin. There were crayon letters on one side. She struggled to read them.

I wanna mum. Dont wanna go way. Sasha luvs me-ask her.

Fear, trepidation and anger all rose in one wave.

"What happened?" she demanded, surging forward to shove him backward into the lounge.

She listened, her face glowering at him, as he related Cody's behavior the night before and remembered how upset the child had been after talking to her. Fear grew as he told her that Cody's bed hadn't been slept in.

"Well, I certainly haven't seen him and I would have. I've been up since five."

He seemed, at last, to notice her silk suit, dressy sandals and makeup. A frown creased his forehead.

"Where are you going so early?" he asked, frowning.

Sasha stood and self-consciously straightened her skirt. "I, er, have an appointment."

"At this hour. Where?" He was staring at her suspiciously, as if she had planned to whisk Cody away from under his nose. She tossed her dark head. Let him wonder.

"I have an appointment in Billings that concerns my future," she told him in a superior voice. "Some of us are not afraid to move ahead in our lives, you know."

Sasha stalked through the gate with great composure. He didn't need to know it was all an act, that she felt nervous and unsure and teary just thinking about taking this inevitable step.

As she slipped the key into the car door her eyes fell on the piece of paper under her windshield wiper. She tugged it out with fear knotting up inside.

Sasha. My dad luvs you. I seed it. Hes just scared.

"You're going to that clinic, aren't you?" She heard the accusing words through a fog and felt his hand jerk her around. "After everything I've said, after the problems you've seen me have raising Cody, you intend to go through with this ridiculous plan, don't you? Answer me.''

Rage, hot and white and billowing, filled Sasha. She surged forward, nose to nose.

"You are a quisling," she stormed. "A niddering. A chicken. A wimp. Shall I expand on that further?" There was no way he could misunderstand her words, she decided. "I love you. And I love Cody. And you know it.'' She glared into his glittering silver eyes and dared him to deny it.

"And we both know darned well that regardless of what I told those silly old farts at church yesterday, you knew perfectly well exactly who you were kissing that night.''

When his eyelids drooped before hers, she felt exultation fill her tired heart as she shoved Cody's latest missive at him.

"Cody's right. You do love me. But you're afraid to deal with that, to take on all the joy and happiness and pain and misery that love might bring.'' She smacked his shoulder in frustration. "Fool! You've got a real live woman whose knees go weak when you kiss her and you're worried that you won't be able to handle it.'' Her tone was scathing.

"Go ahead, Reverend. Admit it. I won't hold you to it. It won't cost you anything. There's no one around to hear.'' She smiled at him bitterly. "Just for once admit the truth. You love me as much as I love you.''

He stood, glaring at her, but immobile.

"Well, Mr. Strong and Silent. What are you afraid of? I already know all about fear. I'm scared every single day that I'll bring this child into the world and botch the job. I'm scared he'll turn out to hate me for not knowing who his father is. I'm scared I won't be able to handle night feedings and fevers and childhood diseases.'' She drew in a lungful of air and hid her shaking hands behind her.

"I'm bloody well petrified that I'll screw this up so badly

that I'll spend the rest of my life regretting this decision,
you big jerk. And it's all your fault.''

The enormity of her decision combined with the tension
of seeing Jake before she took this last major step, hit her
between the eyes and Sasha burst into loud sobbing tears,
aching for a love she would never know from a man who
couldn't admit to a love she knew he felt.

A long silence dragged between them until she heard his
voice, soft and quiet but confident.

''You're not afraid of anything, Sasha Lambert. Not me,
not Cody. Not even Bobby the Brat. You charge into life
ready to tackle anything in your path. You stand up for
what you believe in and you refuse to take no for an answer.''

She felt his arms curve around her waist as he turned her
tear-stained face toward him. His mouth dropped to caress
hers as his hands smoothed over the silky black strands.

''I think that's why I love you so much. You don't let
anyone or anything hold you back from what you want.''

She stopped crying, rubbing at her eyes with one fist.
''What did you say?''

Jake's chest filled with air as he stood staring at her.

''I said,'' he muttered in a rush, kissing her lips. ''I love
you.'' He kissed her ear. ''I love the way you rush to my
rescue when you think I need a champion.'' He kissed her
neck. ''I love the way you look after Cody's best interests.''
His mouth moved to her forehead.

''I love the way you tease and cajole and boss and order
people around until you get them moving again.'' His lips
covered hers and Sasha breathed a sigh of ecstasy. Nothing
had changed. It still felt wonderful. She kissed him back,
glorying in the freedom to touch and feel him so near.

''I don't boss or order anyone,'' she muttered when his
mouth moved to the side of her chin.

''Yes, you do. And then you pretend you had nothing to
do with it when they obey. But that's okay.'' He smiled

down at her. "I love that, too. And I'm just as scared as you are. I've already botched one relationship. I'm not sure I know how to have another. But even that doesn't stop me from loving you."

"Really? You're not just saying it because I made you mad." She studied his face seriously.

He laughed.

"Sweetheart, I've been mad at lots of people lately, but I haven't told one of them that they feel great in my arms. And I've certainly never done this."

His mouth moved masterfully over hers again, drawing a response she couldn't possibly deny.

"Jake?" She tried to focus her eyes, to regain some sense of the scene in front of her.

"Hmm," he murmured, nuzzling her neck. "You smell so good."

"Jake!" She pushed him back. "What about Cody?"

He moaned, dragging his arms away from her pliant body. A look of pain crossed his face as he stared into her eyes. "I think he's run away," he whispered. "And I'm the reason why. Again. Oh, Sasha, I'm so afraid. What am I going to do?"

Sasha hugged him fiercely to her body. "We'll find him," she promised. "And we'll tell him together that we love him. You just have to have faith."

"He'd be so excited if he knew about us. All he's wanted since we moved here was a family." Jake smiled tightly, hanging on to her hand tensely. "He didn't have to run away at all. He's got what he wanted right here."

"Dad, I want you to get married. You can't get married if you don't ask first," a little voice chirped. They whirled around to see Cody leaning against the side of the car, Oreo nuzzling his leg.

"When Mrs. Garner helped me spell the message she said the man's always s'posed to ask the lady if she wants to marry him. It's ness...nesse... You gotta ask, Dad."

Sasha felt a bubble of laughter tickle her. He was so darn cute! Jake, however, was not so easily swayed.

"Where have you been, Cody? I've been worried sick. I thought you had run off when I didn't find you in bed this morning." He knelt and met the little boy's gaze with his own. "Son?"

"Well, I was gonna go away to Aunt Janice's but I 'cided it was too far away. So I came over to Sasha's, and me an' Oreo slept in the car. It was cool!"

Jake, hands raking wildly through his hair, looked about to erupt with wrath at the little boy's calm explanation. Sasha touched his arm gently and shook her head. Moving in front of him, she lifted the boy onto the hood of the car and smiled softly.

"Well, Cody, it wasn't cool for your dad or me. We love you and we were really worried about you. That's one thing people who love each other are pretty careful about, you see. We think about the other person and how much we might hurt them."

Cody nodded. "I know it. Just like friends do, like me an' Bobby." His head tipped to one side as he watched his dad slip an arm around Sasha's waist. "Are we gonna be a family, Dad?"

Jake grinned down at his son and winked. His eyes were shining with satisfaction as they smiled at her. Sasha decided he was the most handsome man she had ever seen.

"Well, son. I haven't actually proposed yet, you understand. But if you and I ask her really nicely, I think Sasha might help us be a big, happy family."

Cody stared up at Sasha inquiringly. "Well?" he demanded finally. "Has my dad got enough love now, Sasha?"

"Yes," she murmured. "I think he's got enough for both of us, Cody." Sasha hugged the little boy to her heart.

Satisfied that life was progressing as it should, Cody wandered over to feed the dog.

"I still want a child," Sasha whispered to Jake, holding up her envelope of pertinent information from the clinic. "Do you want to come with me?"

He plucked it out of her hands and tossed it into the nearby trash barrel before tugging her into his arms.

"Why, Miss Lambert! Whatever would the congregation think of such a scandalous proposition? Our children are going to have two parents, I'm adamant about that." He kissed her then, in plain view of the neighbors and Cody and God. "But I promise that I'll be right there by your side, ready to help, if you promise to stay by mine. Got it?"

"Not quite," Sasha murmured dreamily. "Could you tell me it all again?"

The whole town was there, crowded into the confines of the tiny church, waiting for the bride to emerge. That was what they'd decided upon.

"We can't exclude anyone," Sasha had informed Jake. "There would be hard feelings. And anyway, in some ways they've all had a part in this."

Jake had tightened his grip on her waist and nuzzled the soft skin of her neck with his lips.

"Well," he'd growled into her ear, "they can come to the wedding. And they're welcome at the reception. But after that, they go. For once we're going to have some privacy." He'd kissed her then, hard and demanding. "And no one is going to interrupt us again until I say so."

Sasha had laughed and drawn back a bit.

"You spoke too soon, darling." She'd giggled. "Here comes the ring bearer now."

Jake had merely tugged her tighter into his embrace. "This is my time," he'd complained loudly. "Let him get his own woman."

Cody grinned at the sight of his dad and soon-to-be mom.

"Akshully, I met Sasha first." His eyes twinkled up at his dad, copper freckles dancing on his jubilant face. "But it's okay. You can keep kissin' her. I don't mind at all."

As he wandered off to watch his favorite television program, Jake and Sasha looked at each other and grinned.

"A very intelligent boy, my son." Jake had grinned. "Wonderful sense of timing."

Sasha had merely tugged his head down to hers for another kiss. If she wasn't mistaken, Sasha had mused as her fiancé's mouth closed over hers, that child was operating on a hidden agenda.

She still thought it today—on her wedding day.

Sasha listened as Mrs. Natini pressed the loud pedal a little harder, obviously hoping to cover some of the boisterous discussion in the congregation.

"She's a real gem of a wife for a minister," Flora Brown whispered loudly. "Types faster than I do, too, which is a real blessing considering that man's handwriting."

"Having a wife that can do all those craft things will be a real help to the girls' club. She's got more talent in her little finger than I have in this whole body." The church club leader nodded her head in satisfaction.

"I heard she made the dress herself," Mrs. Bratley whispered, one hand closed tightly around Bobby's wriggling form as she held him in place and inclined her head toward Bobby's father. "Purest satin, they say."

Mrs. Garner turned right around in her pew to eye them both with disfavor. "Not satin, Vera. It's silk—peau de soie." She gave the words a foreign inflection that had the other two nodding.

"Pastor Jacob looks good, doesn't he, Esther?" Flora inclined her head toward the tall, handsome groom standing at the front. "She's perked him up some."

The ladies all nodded in approval at the elegant black-suited figure standing tall and lean at the front of the church.

The organ sounded then, a loud trumpeting call that had everyone standing for the bridal march. First down the aisle was Deidre. The entire congregation gasped at the vividness of her rich purple gown. Following her, Janice Armstrong moved regally past. Her stern face was wreathed in smiles as she looked toward the altar where her brother stood waiting.

Next Cody strode through the door importantly, holding his arm out for Kate to hang on to. He whispered a few words to the little girl before the couple moved slowly down the aisle. Everyone heard her disgusted reply.

"I already *know*, Cody."

And then Sasha was moving through the entrance.

A collective gasp went up as the tall regal figure swayed, stepping slowly down the aisle, silk skirts rustling as she moved. It had taken hours to make the dress and not a few tears. But Sasha was pleased with the way the sheer top left her shoulders and arms exposed before meeting with the bodice to plunge into a daring vee, the slanted line repeated at the waist. Slim and flaring gently, the skirt fell to the floor in a smooth drape of purest silk that accentuated her height and left a long train of floating white tulle behind. It was a simple style but very elegant, showing her height and well-endowed figure to greatest advantage.

Her veil was shoulder-length with a few seed pearls scattered over it, held in place by a tiny Juliet cap. Old—that was her shoes, borrowed from Deidre. New—her beautiful ring from Jake. Borrowed—her mother's pearl earrings. Blue—a homemade garter Cody had insisted she wear.

Sasha kept her head up and focused on her bridegroom through the blurred folds of her veil. With each step his face grew more distinct. There was no mistaking the gleam of love in his eyes, or the smile on his dark face. She stopped just long enough to hand her mother one of the irises from her bouquet before stepping up beside him.

His big warm hand closed over hers.

"Fantastic! Most salubrious," was what he murmured, stealing her word for the day. But his eyes spoke volumes. "What's with the purple bridesmaid dresses? They look like your couch." His voice came hissing through her veil.

"I thought you said grape was your favorite color," she whispered with a perfectly straight face.

"I said grape bubblegum, not the color grape."

The minister was waiting to begin, but Sasha just had to wipe that sour look off Jake's dark face.

"Oh, sorry," she murmured in tones for his ears only. "I didn't know that and I bought a grape negligee for tonight."

"I like grape. It's my very favorite color." A sunny smile lightened his gloomy features. She blushed at the innuendo in his words.

They recited the age-old vows in front of their friends and neighbors, pressing the golden bands into place with a promise.

"Sasha, I pledge my eternal love to you and promise that I will always be there when you need me. I will trust in you and believe in you and lean on you as you lean on me. You will be my forever love."

His silvery eyes shone as he said the words and she swallowed the lump that rose in her throat at his tender voice. With shaking hand, Sasha bent to slip her ring from Cody's pillow and slid it over Jake's finger before offering her own pledge.

"Jake, I love you and promise you that I will be by your side for the rest of our journey through life. I vow to love you and honor you and help you regardless of where that journey leads. And I promise not to incur any future opprobrium."

"There she goes again with those crazy words," Marv Seever complained to his wife in a loud whisper. "What does the woman mean?"

"Disgrace him," Sasha enunciated loudly. She turned

and grinned at the elderly board member. Then, bending, she spoke directly to Jake's son in a soft voice meant for him alone. "And I promise you that you will always be my son, Cody. I will always love you. No matter what."

Cody grinned. "Is this where you kiss my dad?" he whispered loudly.

The congregation laughed heartily.

"Not yet, son," Pastor Dan murmured. He winked down at the boy. "But soon." With a few timeless words he united them for eternity. "Okay, Cody. Now."

"You may kiss the bride," Cody crowed. "Only I should say, my mom." His chest puffed out with pride. And the groom followed his son's excellent advice to the thunderous applause of his parishioners.

Jake and Sasha floated back down the aisle and stood on the steps to receive the good wishes of the townsfolk. Someone showered them in confetti, which was strictly forbidden on church grounds, but somehow acceptable when it was the minister and his new wife who were being sprinkled.

They endured the quirky little stories and jokes at their expense. They enjoyed the seemingly endless rounds of tinkling crystal that signaled yet another heated kiss and they reveled in the goodwill and hearty congratulations their parishioners bestowed on them.

Sasha drew Cody near as, together, the three of them opened the lovely gifts their friends had so thoughtfully brought to start their new life together. Then there was a special smile and a hug for each as friends and neighbors received their portion of the very ornate cake Deidre had provided.

Finally, after tossing the bridal bouquet, Sasha and her preacher clambered into Jake's battered Jeep, its rear bumper decorated with a trail of cans and a crudely lettered sign that said Just Married.

"Where are you off to?" Deidre called, holding Sasha's

bouquet with pride. She grinned as her friend merely shrugged her elegantly clad shoulders.

"I don't know," Sasha admitted. Her wide mouth curved upward fondly as she climbed into the car. "But I think Cody does. He and Jake have been whispering all week long."

"It's a seecrud," Cody reminded her. His mouth split into a happy grin. "And I ain't telling nobody. 'Cause moms and dads need time to be alone together."

The entire crowd waved and cheered as the pastor and his wife drove down the street and out onto the highway. And no one cared when a few afternoon droplets fell from the darkening skies. They simply went back inside to celebrate the wedding of the year in Allen's Springs.

Cody was chatting a mile a minute as he returned to his glass of red punch.

"I think Sasha's gonna love Paris. My dad said she thinks it's roma..." He stopped and thought for a moment before shaking his dark head. His freckles danced as he looked up at Deidre. "Anyway, Dad said she'd like it. An' I don't mind," he confided. "'Specially if they're getting me that brother." He grinned happily.

Suddenly he yanked on Deidre's purple skirt. She bent her head nearer the dark shiny one.

"Do you think that it takes a lot of work to get a new brother?" His brow furrowed in concern.

Deidre peered out the window at the tiny speck of dust that told her how fast the departing couple were traveling. Her mouth creased into a smile.

"Yep," she agreed. "A whole lot of work." Her eyes narrowed mischievously and she grinned with smug satisfaction.

"But I think your parents are up to it, Cody."

* * * * *

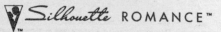

Catch more great

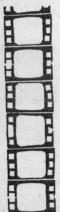

HARLEQUIN™ Movies

featured on the movie channel tmc

Premiering May 9th
The Awakening

starring Cynthia Geary and
David Beecroft, based on the novel by
Patricia Coughlin

Don't miss next month's movie!
Premiering June 13th
Diamond Girl
based on the novel by bestselling author
Diana Palmer

If you are not currently a subscriber to
The Movie Channel, simply call your
local cable or satellite provider for more
details. Call today, and don't miss out
on the romance!

100% pure movies.
100% pure fun.

Makes any time special™

An Alliance Television Production

The World's Most Eligible Bachelors are about to be named! And Silhouette Books brings them to you in an all-new, original series....

World's Most
Eligible Bachelors

Twelve of the sexiest, most sought-after men share every intimate detail of their lives in twelve never-before-published novels by the genre's top authors.

Don't miss these unforgettable stories by:

Dixie Browning

Marie Ferrarella

Jackie Merritt

Tracy Sinclair

BJ James

Rachel Lee

Suzanne Carey

Gina Wilkins

VICTORIA PADE

Maggie Shayne

Anne McAllister

Susan Mallery

Look for one new book each month in the **World's Most Eligible Bachelors** series beginning September 1998 from Silhouette Books.

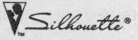

Available at your favorite retail outlet.

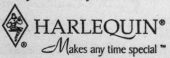

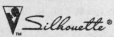

SOMETIMES BIG SURPRISES COME IN SMALL PACKAGES!

Celebrate the happiness that only a baby can bring in **Bundles of Joy** by Silhouette Romance!

February 1998
On Baby Patrol by Sharon De Vita (SR#1276)
Bachelor cop Michael Sullivan pledged to protect his best friend's pregnant widow, Joanna Grace. Would his secret promise spark a vow to love, honor and cherish? Don't miss this exciting launch of Sharon's *Lullabies and Love* miniseries!

April 1998
Boot Scootin' Secret Baby by Natalie Patrick (SR#1289)
Cowboy Jacob Goodacre discovered his estranged wife, Alyssa, had secretly given birth to his daughter. Could a toddler with a fondness for her daddy's cowboy boots keep her parents' hearts roped together?

June 1998
Man, Wife and Little Wonder by Robin Nicholas (SR#1301)
Reformed bad boy Johnny Tremont would keep his orphaned niece at any price. But could a marriage in name only to pretty Grace Marie Green lead to the love of a lifetime?

And be sure to look for additional BUNDLES OF JOY titles in the months to come.

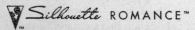

Find us at your favorite retail outlet.

Look us up on-line at: http://www.romance.net

SRBOJF-J